CW01466993

The Fragility of Existence

The first of the
'Fragility' series

A Science Fiction/Apocalyptic novel

By Paul Money

Cover artwork 2023:
Principal Designer ASP

'Earth' original artwork © David Swaby
Based on an original idea by Paul Money

2023 Cover (background image of part of
Cygnus and Moon image) © Paul
Money/Astrospace

The Fragility of Existence

Copyright Notice

Astrospace Publications
18 College Park, Horncastle, Lincolnshire LN9 6RE
England/UK
www.astrospace.co.uk

Language: UK English

Acknowledgements

The author would like to acknowledge the support and help of his wife, Lorraine, in listening to the idea of the novel, how it developed and giving both invaluable advice, encouragement and editing ideas as the story progressed.

He would also like to thank the following for their advice, informed wisdom, patience and encouragement regarding this novel:

Julian Onions
Peter Rea
Pete Williamson

Preface

The extermination of our species was probably inevitable when you look back with hindsight.

Every advanced civilisation has always wiped out the resident less advanced occupants whenever they came into contact.

So it was the same for us, Homo Sapiens.

But it wasn't supposed to have happened.

We were not to know that though.
Perhaps that is a good thing.

For the Universe...

The warning…

Let this be a warning to you.
Yes you!
I'm talking to you from a position of knowledge,
sheer fright, shock and helplessness.

If only we had broken free from superstition.
If only we had seen past race, colour, creed,
superstition.
If only we had united as one planet…

But we didn't.

We didn't even have any time to realise our
faults and mistakes and do something about
them.
We didn't stand a remote 'cat in hells'
chance.

When they came.

This is my warning to you.

Don't ignore it…

1: So, it started like this…

Let me tell you a story…

It's my story really, but concerns all of us, I really do mean all of us, on the planet Earth.

It was actually a fairly average day when all was said and done. Simone and I had each taken a day off work as the weather presenter had said the coming day would be fine with lovely sunshine all day, it would be *really lovely*. So that's what we did and met up with our friends from a couple of streets down the hill from where we live.

Except it rained didn't it! OK, not all day but for a large part of it.

Something to do with the weak front turning out to be not so weak after all and colliding with some other front which itself had strengthened then, oh whatever - you get the idea!

So much for the weather forecast!

Charming, but as Brits, we still got on with enjoying ourselves at the coast. Anderby Creek of all places but hey, it's our coast and we all love it whatever. So, Jason, Caron, Simone and I laughed at the weather and still messed about on the beach despite the warm rain drifting down and soaking us.

The 'Cloud Observatory' glimmered with the multitudes of raindrops spattered all over it and it looked a little sorry for itself but at least it was living up to its name as we wandered around it.

We must have looked like idiots. If there had been anybody else to see us. Bet the locals thought so but they were conspicuously absent.

Oh no, most people had enough common sense to either be at work, indoors or at home in the warm on a day like that, but not us.

We were made of sterner stuff, or so we told each other. We laughed, ran along the beach in the pouring rain and tried to play football but it was too wet. We came off the beach and headed down the coast to Skegness for the so-called amusement arcades and wasted loose change for a while before heading down the almost deserted high street.

On the pavement we spotted a sad solitary figure wandering along and it was plain he was wearing a placard. Sure enough as we got closer we couldn't help but start laughing and trying to stifle rude comments as we read:

It's coming sooner than you think.
The End of the world is almost here.
Repent now and be saved for all eternity.

Err, right, yep, sorry but one of those nutters who couldn't seem to exist in the real world. Not without having to convince people that for the umpteenth time the s*** was going to hit the fan and it was all going to be over.

Unless of course you did what the final line stated:

Join us and be saved from the sins of the world.

Oh, brother did we give him some stick, but he just shook his head, muttered something under his breath, walked off into the distance.

He disappeared around a corner just as the light rain turned a little heavier.

To be fair, it was Jason and I that had done most of the mickey taking and Simone and Caron both berated us for being awful to the chap. I'm sorry, if you are going to go around trying to *frighten* people into joining your particular church, faith or whatever, then you should be ashamed of yourself. Especially if you peddle such nonsense as the world ending. Who can forget the hubbub over the year 2012 when, prior to it, some so called prophets misread the Aztec calendar implying that the world was due to end that year?

Yet here we were several years later.

It was quite simple really, when our calendar ends on December 31st what do you do? Buy another calendar! It's just the Aztecs expected to be around and would have produced another calendar. They didn't know they'd be effectively wiped out. They didn't see that coming did they?

Well, to be fair, neither did we…

Anyhow, Simone and Caron were pals since school, Jason and I had been best buddies since we first bumped into each other at primary school and, yes, it was usually us two that were the ones that got into trouble. Nothing too serious you understand, we weren't that bad.

We just liked playing the fools and playing pranks on those around us who we could get away with doing so. Into so called adulthood and our early twenties, it was at Caron's wedding to Jason that I had met Simone and fallen in love. Not that she noticed at first.

That's the way it goes sometimes, isn't it?

But something clicked between us on a subliminal level and eventually we too got hitched. That was just over eight years ago and six years since we discovered she had a faulty gene that prevented her bearing children.

OK, so we discussed it over and over, but we were both of the opinion that if we couldn't have any naturally then we wouldn't do IVF or adopt. Our choice, probably just as well considering what was about to happen, but I get ahead of myself. Where was I? Oh yes…

Anyway, we were godparents to Caron and Jason's offspring, seven-year-old Timothy and his six-year-old sister, the very bossy, Samantha They were enough to keep anyone busy and it must be said we did enjoy child minding once in a while to give their parents a break.

We naturally spoiled the kids rotten much to their parents' chagrin.

So that fateful day we left Caron and Jason to go and pick up their offspring from Caron's parents down in Boston. We headed home after calling in and getting fish and chips for tea, plus a few cans to unwind with before getting back to work the next day.

All was well.

The news must have been a bit slow during the day as all they could concentrate on was a few odd sightings in the sky - possibly meteors. 'Shootings stars', Simone informed me that they are actually the same thing, but who cares? We hadn't noticed anything due to the awful weather that wasn't supposed to be, perhaps there was a link?

The Fragility of Existence

Mind you perhaps the warning signs were there as these things could be seen in daylight and I always thought they were mainly a nighttime thing but hey ho, I wasn't to know, was I?

We went to bed and promptly fell asleep blissfully unaware of what was happening ever closer to us…

Oh, I forgot to introduce myself, I'm Mathew, Matt to everybody except my parents and this is my story…

2: Shock

We really must have had too many cans of the good stuff the previous night.

I slowly came awake, if that's what you could call it, and swore that I could hear screams and even church bells. Was that an aircraft sound? It didn't sound right at all. It was a faint and seemingly distant cacophony of noise. Then I realised that our nearest neighbour tended to have their bedroom windows open even on the coldest night. We sometimes could hear whatever he was watching or even playing, he was into online gaming in a big way apparently, loser or what!

I turned over as Simone snorted in her sleep and I chuckled to myself as I looked at her face bathed in the gentle glow of our night lights.

I dropped off to sleep again.

For a few minutes.

I awoke suddenly, jolted upright as the, by now really loud noises from outside, began to assault my ears and Simone also sat up quite bleary eyed. She suddenly came wide awake at a loud bang in the distance.

"What the hell is going on Matt? Bloody neighbour, I'll give him what for!" She said as she leapt out of bed and stormed towards the window and threw the curtains wide. Forgetting, mind you, that she was stark naked.

She stood there and I looked up at her, faintly illuminated by our small glowworm nightlights we both had taken a fancy to and admired her sleek figure.

Then she was lit up brilliantly and she stepped back and began to shake.

Convulse more like, and I leapt out of bed and held her trying to make sense of her reaction. But the sheer look of terror on her face told volumes and I saw her normally staid, *tough as a nut* constitution, melt as her face was lit up by another flash and I turned to look out the window.

"Oh shit!"

Seems a bit mild when I think about it as I looked out towards Woldsfield, our village. We had a nice spot almost halfway up a shrub and wooded hill overlooking the large village. Woldsfield was actually a new 'garden village' so didn't really have the sort of history most doomsday book age places had.

But it was on fire.

Lots of them!

Something was flitting about both in the sky and moving through the urban landscape. There was destruction on a scale that I can honestly say I'd only ever seen in movie reels of recent conflicts in faraway foreign lands. It reminded me of the big screen action movies where normally, at some late point, the hero's turn the tables on the enemy after much death and destruction and ultimately save the day.

It didn't look like any hero's had turned up.

At least not yet.

Things, that's all I can describe them as, things, were dropping from the sky down into the streets and rapidly moving through them. I gazed out in shock but being a mathematical sort of chap, I spotted a pattern within moments.

They, whoever they were, were systematically moving through and taking out upper floor windows or in some cases snatching up what appeared to be people fleeing for their lives and being thrown into a container following behind.

Dark, sinister shapes…

War of the frigging worlds came to mind and I shuddered at the actual similarity.

It was terrifying.

"Shit!" I said under my breath again.

I rushed into the next room and grabbed my fancy electronic zoom binocular, dashed back into the bedroom to the window and scanned the scenes of devastation before us.

It was unreal.

From our vantage point we could see across the Lincolnshire Wolds and my mind turned to Lincoln, the county capital city. I swept the binocular round along the horizon but all over the place there was a dull red glow and I realised that there were many places on fire. I stopped suddenly and gasped as I had stumbled upon Lincoln Cathedral, only for a large flash to temporarily blind me, then, as my sight returned, I realised there was nothing there.

No cathedral, large swathes of Lincoln were simply gone…

I spotted what seemed to be a jet fighter spin out of control and crash in a ball of flames to the northeast of the city and I could only watch in despair.

I swept back round to Woldsfield.

Something caught my attention and I homed in on a familiar spot.

A familiar street.

A familiar house.

And watched as whatever the things were, had reached it and dragged our friends, Jason, Caron, Timothy and Samantha out and literally threw them into the container behind the craft.

Staring in stunned disbelief, I took in a sharp intake of breath.

There was no way they could have survived that. I retched my heart out as Simone tried to help me and try to figure out what I'd seen but something inside of me kicked into high gear. I spat out the crap in my mouth and swallowed hard to gain control.

It was a foul taste but that was nothing on what I had seen.

"Right, no discussion, quick, grab some clothes, keep the curtains closed and follow me, love." Simone knew from my tone that this was no time for a debate and she hurriedly did as I asked and scooped up our clothes from where we'd chucked them on the chairs by the dresser. I dashed back onto the landing and frantically thought of where we could hide. It seemed futile trying to run at this stage as I figured whoever they, or what they were, would probably be able to spot that and indeed it would make their sickening task presumably easier.

No. Instinct was telling me to hide. It looked like it was a snatch and grab situation with a quick move on to the next house or home. So, as I contemplated this, in what was really just a fraction of a second, my eyes fell on the upper storage cupboard next to the hot water tank cupboard.

The Fragility of Existence

I flung the door open and remembered, as I spotted them, that it held our large suitcases for our holidays abroad.

My wild guess was that in their haste whoever they were would not look high but rather, low, so I grabbed the cases, pulling them out frantically before stacking them neatly under the bed in the spare bedroom at the back. At least I hoped it would make it look like that was where they always belonged.

I sized the space up. Yes, two people could just fit in there and, as I heard a crash that sounded a little too close for comfort, I saw Simone come back in with some clothes. She was shaking and looked terrified.

Who wouldn't be under the circumstances?

I quickly realised we didn't have time to dress so I took them from her and put them on the washing pile in the bathroom.

I beckoned for her to use me to climb up into the storage space. She hesitated then we heard another crash even nearer and she bolted up into the space and wriggled her cute form into it. I looked round then had a thought and rushed back into the bedroom. I spotted my smart phone and dashed back into the spare room and quickly found what I was looking for.

A smartphone endoscope. I'd used it a couple of times to look for things that had dropped into awkward and tight places but now it was going to have another purpose if we survived the next few hours.

I reached up as I used the stair banister to give me a little leverage and with Simone's hands outstretched, she hauled me up into the tight space.

Snug as two bugs.

Somehow, I managed to pull the door closed tight then wondered how the hell we were going to get out as there was no handle on the inside, but it was too late to change minds.

Under certain circumstances it would have been quite sexy really, two naked lovers crammed together in such a confined space, but not at this moment as we heard a tremendous crash and felt the whole house shake.

They had arrived….

3: Tale of two couples

The whole house shook again, and we heard something scramble along the hallway and sound as if it went into the back spare bedroom.

We held our breath and I felt something trickle onto my shoulder and run down my arm.

Simone was crying floods but was somehow too terrified to make a noise. I wriggled a little and managed to kiss her on the cheek, well, I hope it was her cheek, I thought with a wry, but scared witless, mind.

It seemed to be an eternity, clearly something was scrambling through the house, up and down the stairs, but after some noise it all went quiet. Finally, I listened carefully with bated breath as whatever it was went back into the master bedroom and presumably out the shattered front window.

The house fell eerily silent.

Being in such close confines with the love of my life wrapped so tight to me, I was struggling a bit to breathe, but even though common sense suggested who/whatever it was had now left, there was no way I was going to venture out just yet.

No, stay put and wait.

We listened with bated breath but couldn't tell you how long we were up there. I dared not activate my phone as the screen would have lit up the inside of our hiding place and possibly betrayed our location if whatever 'they' were, were still around. My gut instinct kept telling me, 'smash and grab', 'smash and grab'.

The chances were that they'd gone on to the other properties nearby, shit, Mike and Sarah were next door, but what could we have done? There'd been no time to warn them.

I couldn't have chanced it.

We had a detached house with three others along our road which backed onto a shrub filled hill before turning into woodland. I had another suspicion however and it was bugging me as we stayed crammed in that storage cupboard. They could have a second sweep to mop up stragglers. That's how I'd organise something like this.

How long to wait? That was the question.

However, nature has a habit of reminding you that you are mortal and have certain needs.

The cans we'd got through earlier that evening were now wanting to make their exit. My bladder was starting to give me that feeling but I managed to put it to one side. Something else took over as well, fatigue.

So, despite the conditions and circumstances both of us must have fallen into a troubled and fitful sleep.

#

Meanwhile, over at our neighbours at number 12 they too were stirring and beginning to wonder what was going on.

Mike leapt out of bed and carefully peeked out through a gap in the curtains and his heart fair leapt into his mouth. Stunned he struggled to take in what was happening and backed away as Sarah shook her sleepy head and looked bleary eyed at him.

"Wassup? Not that damned neighbour playing his all-night games again is it? You'll have to have words with him. See if Matt will go with you as I bet him and Simone are just as pissed off as we are.

Mike?

Mike, what is it?"

Sarah climbed out of bed as Mike kept shaking his head and mumbling something, she realised it was a prayer. She peeked through the curtain and took in a sharp intake of breath.

Then said one of her own.

Mike looked stunned and frozen with fear, she knew she had to take control of the situation.

"Hide. We need to hide, things are happening too fast out there, quick, drop the loft ladder down and we'd best get up there and hope whatever it is isn't too thorough."

She looked at her husband of forty-three years and saw something she'd never seen before, genuine fear, he was frozen to the spot. Frighteningly mesmerised by the scenes of destruction he was witnessing. They didn't have time for this, she thought and slapped him lightly on the face and he shook his head in shock and surprise. She didn't give him time to say anything.

Sarah pushed past and opened the bedroom door to the landing, stepped over to the far corner and grabbed the long-hooked staff. She pulled at the small slot in the loft door in the landing ceiling and it slid open as the ladder unfolded down to meet them.

She heard a crash too close for comfort. "Oh hell, that has to be Matt and Simones', Mike, SHIFT IT!" And she scurried up the ladder ignoring the fact she was in her nightie.

Mike heard another crash and he broke out of his frozen shocked state and bolted up after her, grabbing his dressing gown in the process. Then just before he pulled the loft door up closed, he had a thought and leant down and managed to grab the hook, pulling it up and throwing it past Sarah as he pulled the loft door closed and it clicked into place.

An almighty bang ricocheted through the loft as their front bedroom windows were smashed in and something began clumsily rummaging through the house.

They stayed silent in pure fear and dread of being found and Mike offered up another silent prayer for not just themselves, but their families, friends and neighbours. It was a nightmare come true and all he could think about was how he'd always enjoyed the sort of movies that showed just the sort of thing that was happening right now. Of course, in the movies, there were always the heroes who saved the day, and all usually ended well.

But this was reality, not a movie. He shuffled around as quietly as best he could and sought out Sarah's hand as they waited holding their breaths uncertain if they were going to be discovered or not, he hoped.

#

Our house, number 11

My eyes slowly opened, for a brief moment I was disoriented, then I realised what had happened and that I could faintly see some form of light filtering under the door.

Simone stirred and I realised my whole body was cramped as she had somehow ended up on the top of me. Not surprising considering the close confines. Under other circumstances that would have been very pleasurable.

But not today.

My bladder also woke up, but I clenched and forced the feeling away. I listened intensely for any sound that might signal our imminent discovery, but no sound stirred. Indeed, I realised that not even the fridge freezer was making any noise.

Power must be off.

Bathroom! The urge had come back.

I had an idea and managed to shuffle enough to move the smart phone into a position where I could see it in the weak light. The endoscope attachment was still in place - I had thought it would have dropped off but now it was going to have its most important role. I activated the phone and twisted my finger enough to touch the right app symbol on the screen and sure enough the screen sprang to life with a view from the endoscope.

Again, under different conditions the view would have been fun as the mini light illuminated part of Simone's left breast and she snorted as quietly as she could. I realised she was able to look over my shoulder at the screen, but I quickly moved the phone and 'scope down to the base of the door and tried to push it under and into the gap.

Success!

The screen blanked out briefly then adjusted to the daylight and I could make out the landing and stairs.

Dust and some debris, presumably from the front bedroom covered the floor with a few flashes from what must have been shards of glass. I twisted the endoscope probe and gradually got a feel for the lie of the land. The front bedroom door had wafted shut, probably from the now open to the air, front windows being smashed in.

That was a good sign and, as I scanned the landing, I looked for any sign for something out of the ordinary. I heaved a sigh of relief on not seeing anything strange left behind that could have been a warning system.

"Well?" Came a hushed voice close to my right ear. "I need the loo, I'm bursting!"

That made two of us then!

"Listen." I whispered. "There looks to be bits of glass on the floor but not as much as I feared. I'll open the door and climb down then try to clear the floor a bit so you can drop down. Whatever you do, DON'T FLUSH the loo or make any noise!"

I didn't need to see the scowl on her face as I could mentally feel it!

"OK, understood, not that I'm that daft as it happens. I'll hold on but don't be long as those lagers have reached parts other lagers have never been to before." She whispered back.

If it wasn't such a dire situation then I'd have started to laugh.

Not this morning.

Cautiously pushing against the door, at first it refused to open. I pushed harder and it suddenly gave way and I only just managed to stop myself falling.

Fortunately, I grabbed the banister just in time to stop me treading on a particularly nasty looking bit of glass.

I looked around then poked my head gingerly into the spare room at the back and saw an old dustpan and brush we had come close to throwing out. That would do nicely, I thought to myself and got busy cleaning the floor so that Simone could get down.

I stretched to free up the cramped muscles and as I did so she jumped down then dashed past me and sat on the toilet as she heaved a sigh of utter relief.

All I could think about was how noisy it sounded as her pee hit the water in the bowl and for a moment, I froze listening intently just in case it attracted unwelcome attention.

Nothing, but unfortunately it brought back my own urge and I thought, what the heck, and positioned myself over the bathroom sink and allowed the pee to flow freely.

Simone wrinkled her nose but nodded in understanding and I finished off and carefully ran the tap with just enough of a trickle to allow me to wash the bowl out, then wash my hands. Simone finished off, sighed with relief, and joined me to clean her hands then we both headed into the spare room. I grabbed the clothes we had thrown down on the wash pile in the bathroom and we quickly got dressed.

I didn't notice at the time, but she was hobbling a little and somehow, she managed to keep from wincing as she put her right foot down. She was always the brave one of the two of us.

If only she had said something...

#

Mike and Sarah, number 12

Sarah was drowsy but kept trying to stay awake. It had been almost an hour since the noises in the house had subsided along with the sound of something leaving the house from the shattered windows of the bedroom. They had kept each other awake, just about, but despite the situation Mike was now dropping off to sleep and Sarah was terrified that his habit of snoring would attract unwanted attention.

She pinched him carefully but hard enough to make sure he awoke, and he stuttered into life and scowled briefly at her. She could barely see him with her small torch but knew that the loft conversion had given them a nice bit of extra space and was insulated well, so she didn't think the light would show. The builders were expected back in a week or so's time to set about installing the window extensions into the roof, but she figured that would be on hold until the government got to grips with the situation and regained control.

What was going on and why their new-ish garden village had been targeted was beyond her, but she had full faith in the government and order would soon be restored.

At least, that's what she kept saying to herself, but what she had seen was disturbing to say the least and something deep inside of her was very worried.

At least she and Mike had something good to fall back on and she said a silent prayer knowing that Mike would be doing the same and probably asking for their salvation in the eyes of the Lord.

She knew she had faith that there was a greater plan the good God had in store for them all.

Meanwhile, Mike searched deep inside but from what he'd seen, they would need more than faith if they were to get through the next few days.

He was, for the first time in his life, genuinely scared. But of course, would not openly admit it to Sarah. Too much kept running through his fevered imagination.

Would 'they' come back? Was it already over and they'd been beaten? Where had they come from and why had the good Lord not forewarned them?

He would certainly be taking that last thought up with their local Vicar the next time they went to church, a few days' time on Sunday.

"We'd best stay here until it's daytime. If we wander around the house with the lights on that would be like suicide." He whispered to Sarah and she nodded in the weak light of her torch. She looked at him and smiled as it seemed he had regained his normal workmanlike composure.

"I don't have a signal for my phone, have you?" She whispered back and saw him fish into his dressing gown pocket and pull out his own smart phone.

"No, in fact I have no network either. Wonder if that means whatever it was earlier trashed the router or worse still, power is off."

"Bugger, fridge and freezer may be off then if that's the case." Sarah replied in a hushed tone. She regretted that they had decided to wait until the loft conversion was finished before bringing anything up to furnish it.

Still, with the dust and mess that she expected would be caused when the windows were installed then it had been the right decision at the time.

But now the hardboard flooring was tough to sit on for any length of time and she carefully stood up and stretched her body to relieve the aching muscles. Mike did the same then they hugged as quietly as they could whilst also giving each other support and comfort in this strange time. In many respects it was probably a good thing that the workman had not prepared the way with the windows, otherwise they would have been exposed and visible to whatever it was ransacking their small but beautiful little new village.

They settled down and managed to lie together as best they could and finally fell into a troubled state of sleep.

4: Plans of action

Our house, number 11

"So what the hell are we going to do smart arse?"

I guess Simone could have called me much worse, but she actually meant it in a sort of loving way as we always had a bit of banter between us. That was part of the fun of our marriage when I look back on the years we were together.

I shook my head but then carefully opened a slit in the back-bedroom curtains, just enough of a crack for me to push the endoscope out and look around.

Normal.

That was the surreal thing about the view as we were looking out over the back garden. That in turn backed onto the shrubs on the gentle slope upwards of 'our hill' as we often called it. Not that we had the money to have bought it you understand. Couldn't have done anyway as the locals had managed to preserve it and stop further development and expansion of 'Woldsfield'.

Trees took over, crowning the hilltop. I'd sometimes wondered if they were safe in high winds, but we'd had a storm a couple of years back, one of the worst on record, and they'd stood firm despite the record-breaking winds. I tapped Simone on the shoulder making her jump and I explained my worry that there would be a second 'sweep' looking for stragglers.

Simone nodded dourly as I began to formulate a plan.

"Let me creep downstairs and see what it's like, you find our rucksacks - I reckon we'd best get stocked up with food and a few essentials and then take cover in the woods out back. I'll grab the binoculars as well so we can at least try to look for signs of others or keep a look out for 'them'."

"OK." She paused. "Matt?"

"Yes love?"

"Do you think it's like this all over the world."

I think my silence and worried look gave her the answer. I turned away and carefully, slowly, I crept down the stairs. We'd done the usual, normal thing most people do and closed the curtains before we had headed up to bed a little worse for wear. That was less than twelve hours earlier and I shuddered as I again recalled the horrifying scene, through the binocular, of our friends being tossed into the container.

My heart sank and I felt like crying, had to keep strong, our lives now depended on it. I looked around the darkened hallway at the base of the stairs and turned back towards, and entered, the kitchen.

Yep, the power was off and the fridge/freezer was eerily silent but having been kept closed I figured everything would probably still be fresh. Fresh enough for me to fill a couple of bags anyway.

I looked at its contents and grabbed the fresh veg, bottles of flavoured water (I know, but they taste sooo good!). Most of the veg could be eaten uncooked such as the carrots and peas, the latter being my favourite when the local farmers were pea harvesting. The various sliced meats and cheeses we liked would also keep reasonably fresh if the small freezer packs were still OK.

I bent down and opened the freezer section and a wisp of cool air drifted up and I breathed a sigh of relief seeing the contents were still pretty much frozen. Power could only have been off a few hours at most, I figured.

I crammed what I could into the bags along with several freezer packs and grabbed bread out of the side cupboard but stopped dead in my tracks as I heard a noise outside from the garden.

This was it, the second sweep, but if it was the back garden then we were stuffed with no other route open to us.

There it was again, I cautiously leant over and tried to open up the kitchen curtains just a crack to get the lie of things.

Nothing.

I carefully fished out my smart phone and the endoscope, it was really beginning to pay for itself, I thought with a wry smile. Then I pushed it out between the curtains and watched the screen like a hawk.

There it was again but I could see nothing untoward, so I pulled it back and crept around to the back door, carefully putting the bags down. Grabbing the key off its hook, I slipped it into the keyhole cringing as I thought it made a sound like someone keying a car door for spite, as it clicked on turning. These things do that don't they? Always sound much louder when you want to be as quiet as possible. I held my breath then slowly pushed the door handle and opened the door a fraction and eased the endoscope out through the gap.

Again, nothing seemed out of place but there was the noise again off to the right where the side path met the gate.

I cautiously went out and crept round with apprehension.

A screech and suddenly two cats came hurtling past me fighting and clawing each other as they scrambled across the lawn. They raced through a small gap in the fence, disappearing into the shrubs still growling and snarling at each other as they did so.

I can tell you in all honesty, I think I nearly crapped in my pants! I turned and looked over to Mike and Sarah's but the house looked quiet and, I hoped, they'd somehow managed to get away.

#

Mike and Sarah, number 12

The phone alarm sounded and Mike went to turn over to switch it off ready to get up for another day at the office then as he realised he wasn't in bed. He snatched at it and turned it off as Sarah came awake with a start and looked horrified at him.

They sat on the floor and waited, terrified that the wake-up alarm had not alerted 'them' to where they were hiding and as the long minutes ticked by, every passing second seemed to take an eternity.

What seemed like hours, but was really only twenty or so minutes, nothing had happened, the house appeared silent and slowly they began to relax.

Mike looked sheepishly at Sarah.

"Sorry…" Was all he could say and she looked scathingly at him. But after another half hour even she began to relax.

"Pity they hadn't got stopped by the weather the other week…" She began in a whispered tone, "otherwise we'd have the windows installed up here and we could have peeked out to see if it's all clear."

Mike nodded and motioned to her and towards the loft door in the floor. "I'm going to take a look so just keep quiet and let's see if it is all clear." She looked alarmed but he looked back at her and she relaxed, nodded and decided to put her trust and faith in her husband.

He carefully began to lift the latch and the door started to open but he had forgotten about the ladder mechanism, and it automatically slid out down to the landing floor and both their hearts stopped for a brief moment.

No sound, nothing.

Mike stepped carefully down the ladder casting his eyes warily around so as not to be surprised by anything that might be lurking in wait.

He looked around, noting the debris on the floor including some shards of glass. He was glad of the solid slippers Sarah had given him for his birthday just a few weeks ago. Sixty-four, he only had another few years to go to retirement he mused. It seemed like a distant memory, something that now belonged in another time, a better time than now. He looked up at Sarah keeping watch on him and he carefully stepped along the landing and peeked into the bedroom.

The windows were smashed in and what was left of the shredded curtains fluttered in the open air.

The walls were still intact, but he closed the door as Sarah quickly came down the ladder to join him. He beckoned to her and he slowly headed down the staircase darting his head, looking about, on alert for anything untoward. Apart from various ornaments scattered on the stairs from their display shelves there was nothing amiss.

He reached the bottom and opened the door into the hallway, ready to pull it shut at a moment's notice but still things were all quiet, much to his relief. He heard soft footsteps and knew Sarah was now behind him, she was fearless, that wife of his, he mused, and gave up a brief silent prayer for the Lord bringing them together.

Carefully they moved through the house making sure the curtains stayed closed in the downstairs front and back rooms. The power was off, how long for, was anyone's guess but the fridge and freezer were still cold so at least they would have a source of food.

Sarah quickly busied herself making up a pile of sandwiches and cold drinks as the kettle wouldn't work with no power. She collected together as much edible items without preparation foodstuffs as she could and piled them into plastic containers of all sizes, she knew she'd kept them for a reason!

Mike peered out carefully from the front curtains, but his heart sank at seeing the destruction all down the road extending down into the village they had come to call home.

Woldsfield may have been relatively new but, nestled in the Lincolnshire Wolds, it had been carefully and thoughtfully planned out to be as natural as possible.

He headed back to the kitchen and beckoned to Sarah. "Anything I can do?"

"Get some sheets, blankets, spare pillows and anything else we can put up in the loft in case we have to spend a few days up there. We may as well be as comfortable as possible whilst we wait for the Government to sort out the invaders. Any sign of Matt and Simone?"

"No, house looks deserted, just like the others, do you think…?"

"No, hope not. Doesn't bear thinking about. They were such a lovely couple and that Simone is quite on the ball so with luck they've hopefully escaped." Sarah said, inwardly she had her doubts.

"Hope so, don't know where to though as everything looks so…desecrated." Mike turned and headed back to the staircase and up to rummage round in the spare bedroom and storage units for the blankets.

Sarah continued in the kitchen and, packing everything up she carried the bags upstairs, all the while keeping an ear out listening for signs of humans returning or in case the attackers came back.

They spent the afternoon in the loft but at least were now comfortable and Mike had found their small portable tables usually reserved for days away so they sat and ate in a surreal situation as if they were on a picnic.

But of course, they weren't.

The Fragility of Existence

Late afternoon, Mike headed downstairs carefully to fetch some cushions from the living room. He'd been careful not to open any curtains and with no power for lighting, he had a small pocket torch that he used sparingly and kept it pointed towards the floor so as not to invite attention.

He stopped suddenly.

A sound from the back yard.

He froze for an instant then carefully edged towards the kitchen and peered slowly round.

Nothing. Yet there it was again, a low groan. The hairs began to stand up on the back of his neck but still, he moved towards the back door and opened it slightly, peering through the thin gap. Suddenly two cats tore through the gap in the wooden slatted fence between Matt and Simone's garden and their own and, startled, he fell backwards sending a jug and serving dish crashing to the floor.

The sound seemed loud and horrendous and he panicked and rushed through and up the stairs, up the loft ladder like greased lightening, pulling the loft door shut.

Sarah sat shocked and terrified at the same time.

He leaned over to her and whispered. "Cats outside fighting startled me and I caught your Mum's fancy serving jug and it fell on the floor. I dare not wait around to see if anything heard!"

Sarah looked sternly at him, her Mum's jug was a family heirloom passed down through four generations, but under the circumstances she had to forgive him. Once all this nonsense was over however it would be a different matter, she mused.

The Fragility of Existence

They waited nervously for over an hour but gradually calmed down as nothing happened and there was no sound of anything entering the house.

5: Two fates...

Our house, number 11

Simone held the second rucksack tight to her chest and waited for my signal. It was almost mid evening twilight by my reckoning, and we'd kept hidden at the back of the house with its curtains closed for the we worked out our plan. All the while we listened out for any signs or sounds that could be the aliens returning. The rucksacks were stuffed with the food that I reckoned would last at least several days along with a few simple items of clothing and some sanitary antibacterial gel.

That last was Simone's suggestion as she figured we had no idea if we'd be able to find clean water as we tried to get away from what remained of Woldsfield.

Where could we go?

Well, I'd been thinking about it and to be truthful I felt we were probably doomed but I'd remembered a piece in the local news rag and on local TV at least a year or so earlier.

A famous, well sort of, B or C, maybe even D list celebrity rock singer had bought an old abandoned, and almost forgotten, World War two bunker that lay about a couple of miles from us up in the wooded hills. He'd fought tooth and nail to get permission to turn it into his own private hideaway and its grounds had tall metal fencing erected with only one entrance for vehicles which was all electronically controlled.

At least there should have been a tall metal fence, but local conservationists had successfully stopped him from doing that due to the wood being protected. Despite that, somehow a fence of sorts had been erected in the end.

It had caused an outcry at the time as we all thought the woodland surrounding it was protected but, well, let's just say we reckon money had passed hands and somehow planning permission had been granted for the bunker part. Workman doing the extensive underground refurbishment had probably been given huge sums of money to keep quiet about what was actually done to the old bunker.

One wondered if indeed threats had been made to ruin them, but a TV investigative journalist had tried and failed to get anyone to talk. Speculation had been rife at the time but as the say, money talks.

It was a long shot. Perhaps he was ensconced inside and protected, especially with the woodland all around to help hide what was, on the surface, a small concrete low-level building. If so then what would be the chance if we did indeed make it there? Would he let us in? Would he be violent if we tried to get in? Who knew? Perhaps there were other survivors who had thought along the same lines as me?

Deep down I hoped there were others, surely, we couldn't be the only ones who'd hidden when we realised what was going on? Too many questions, let alone the other big ones: had the whole world succumbed? Did we have anything left of a government? Who the hell were these beings and where had they come from?

The Fragility of Existence

Did we stand a chance against them?

Above all, we, as the supposedly 'intelligent' race on Earth, had not got our act together, wiped out greed, bigotry and hatred for our fellow beings and united as one planet so that we at least could have stood a chance in what now seemed a very frightening universe.

I was tired and Simone and I had gone over and over what we were to do, and we agreed we didn't have much of a choice. It was now late evening, but I kept feeling we had to be on the move soon.

So, I crouched just inside our kitchen door then indicated to Simone to follow. We'd used her smart tablet to save a map of the area as it was clear the entire network was down, no chance of Internet, if it even existed anymore. At another time having no internet might have been a blessing for some people, they would have had to talk to each other!

Carefully opening the back door, we crept along the side of our garage towards the back of the garden then quickly hopped over the fence. I couldn't help thinking that we'd only just had it repaired and improved, seemed a waste now!

Our garden backed onto the slope of the shrub, then wooded, hill. Something flittered into my mind when I remembered we'd asked the council to look into chopping some of the nearby trees down. We thought there was a chance they could topple onto the house if we suffered a similar storm as we'd had just a couple of years earlier, but they refused.

I was glad of that now.

They afforded cover of sorts, especially as it was still late summer, and they had their leaves on.

The Fragility of Existence

I heard Simone say something like 'ouch' and I wondered if she must have caught herself on something as she climbed over our fence. I thought nothing more of it when she just beckoned me to carry on. Perhaps twisted her ankle but I heard something in the distance, and I froze on the spot.

They were coming back for a second sweep just as I had suspected.

Oh brother!

Or words to that effect if you get my drift.

#

Mike and Sarah, number 12

Evening turned to night and now Mike needed the little boys room. "Need to go, back soon. Love you!" He carefully opened the loft door and allowed the ladder to unfold. This time he held on to it to stop it clattering and lowered it down gently before heading down on to the landing then across to the bathroom.

He sat in the darkness with not a sound, well a slight tinkling admittedly. He finished off and cleaned up, walked over to the hand basin and carefully ran the tap with a slight trickle.

Something flashed faintly outside the frosted bathroom window, but he was now lost in deep thought and didn't notice as his mind kept wondering what the Lord, his saviour, had planned for them. He turned and was about to head back to the landing when, absentmindedly he realised he had not flushed the toilet and headed back, instinctively pushing the central plunger for a full flush.

Instantly he did it he felt his heart stop in shock at what he'd done, and he froze listening out for anything untoward.

There were sounds now coming from outside and he finally noticed the flashes from the sky through the frosted glass. In a blind panic he raced through onto the landing and bolted up the loft ladder quickly pulling it shut as the ladder slid to one side in its stowed position.

Sarah didn't need to ask as she'd heard the toilet flush. She sat in silence, terrified, as Mike climbed into the loft and shut the door. He looked at her and his expression cried out that he was sorry, but she just shook her head then had a thought and turned off the torch light.

They sat in silence and darkness, the minutes trickled by as they dared not move for fear of being heard. An hour and slowly they began to relax.

Then they heard it.

Something was now in the house.

Downstairs the four-legged creature was exploring the house it had been assigned to the previous night. It was now being a little more methodical and had a photographic memory. Something had changed as it looked around with its compound eyes spaced around its 'head', for want of a better description. A panoramic continuous view, it stopped and studied the broken remains of what appeared to be a storage container and some form of flattish utensil on the floor.

New.

It remembered where the items had been on a working surface and inside there was satisfaction and a knowing feeling.

The ground floor held nothing further of note, so it clambered up the crude surface that took it to the next level. It wandered into the back room and stopped as it took in the missing sheets and blankets.

New.

Of course, it didn't know what the coverings were called on this horrible world they had come to, but it did know they were no longer there. It had to be an indigenous life form that had been missed the previous night.

That was why they always did two and sometimes three sweeps of an area. There were trillions of its kind, and they swarmed onto a world and stripped it bare of almost all life forms.

Delicious…

It was often in these extra sweeps that they paid more attention to possible hiding places. They knew creatures of any world always tried to hide close by to their 'nest', it was a common habit in almost all the species its kind had encountered. So now it swivelled its head and examined the upper surfaces.

An entranceway of some kind.

It lifted the front two 'legs' exploring the wall carefully then used all four 'legs' with their suckers and began to climb up the wall as quietly as it could.

It tested the strength of the upper surface feeling its way. It was firm enough to take its weight, so it slowly moved along until it was at the edge of the framework of the loft door.

It stopped and waited patiently, silently.

With a false sense of security, in the loft, Mike began to relax.

Although it was pitch black, he knew where Sarah was sat from the faint sound of her shallow breathing.

"Sarah, I think we're alright. I reckon it's gone." He whispered and she fumbled and turned on her torch. She'd not heard anything for what seemed like ages now and she nodded at him and weakly smiled.

Mike shuffled over to her and gave her a hug as he offered up a small prayer for their escape.

He turned to move back over towards the loft hatch but didn't spot the leftover plastic glass. It was sent spinning over the hardboard surface and Mike and Sarah froze in fear, but nothing happened for a brief moment.

Then all hell broke loose…

It heard the sound, triangulated where it had originated, gently probed the ceiling surface then smashed two of its 'legs' through the loft hatch and threw the remains upwards into the space above.

Quick as lightening it shot up into the loft and in a flash two of its retracted upper appendages spooled out and looped round the two terrified beings and then it injected them with the venom.

Quick acting, they both looked in horror as the lower half of their bodies lost sensation then the feeling crept up towards their heads as they slumped to the floor. Mike passed out first, he had been the closest and there had been a fraction of a second difference between them.

Sarah watched, terrified but unable to move as she saw the creature wind in Mike tight to its body.

Then, as she started to lose consciousness, she realised she was being wound in as well.

The venom did its job and enabled the captives to continue to live but in a state of suspended animation, ideal for the feast later…
…with fresh food.

Mike and Sarah's fate had been sealed by a simple plastic glass…

6: Hide!

Simone instinctively held her breath and so did I, but it was unmistakable. In the distance were several strange rumblings, some of it sounded just like the previous night and I wondered if whoever they, or 'it' were, or was using thermal imaging? If so, then somehow we had to mask our body heat signatures and I couldn't help briefly thinking that we were in a scene from a B rated sci fi horror movie.

But this was real life.

What to do?

It was Simone who had the bright spark.

A few hundred metres away on the back of our housing estate there was a large underground pipe. Before the estate was built there was a large drainage ditch and she remembered that when the new 'garden village' was being proposed and then built, to avoid possible flooding of the village, a large pipe was to be installed in its place to ensure water from the local drainage area could still escape and be directed to a large reservoir further downstream.

Local kids had started to play in it until a fateful accident occurred when one of them drowned in just a foot of water. So, where the pipe stopped and again became a ditch the entrance was adapted with a concrete enclosure and a metal access grill at the front of it to allow the water to pass through, but nothing like a child would be able to get in.

But what about an adult?

Could we break into it I wondered?

I beckoned to her and we scrambled along through the undergrowth.

At least there was some overhead protection from the tree leaf cover from air or even space bound spying eyes. As we got a little higher, through the occasional gaps in the foliage I was able to look back down now on Woldsfield and spotted movement, this time covering all sides of each house.

The second wave, as I had suspected.

But they were also quicker and, unnervingly, getting closer to our side of the village. Several times the sky lit up with brilliant flashes and I indicated to Simone not to turn on our small but bright LED torches. Ironic that we'd bought them just for the fact they were small but packed a powerful light. Now if we used them, we'd be spotted instantly.

I heard a groan from Simone and looked back as best I could, but she bumped into me and quietly swore as she muttered about me stopping. The sky was still lighter than I expected, then it hit me, the news had mentioned that tonight would be one of those silly 'supermoon' full Moons. Apparently, the Moons elliptical orbit brought it slightly closer to us than normal and occasionally this happened to coincide with Full Moon. No one seemed to care that every month we have a Full Moon and I had gathered that astronomers did not see it as anything special, in fact just a normal thing, but it had caught the public's attention and fancy.

Now I realised that the sky was still bright because the Moon was rising and adding its light across the land.

Bugger!

Still, after around ten minutes Simone pushed past me and stopped me in my tracks as she had realised, we were close to the pipe's entrance.

In the dim light, occasionally lit up by what the aliens were doing to the village, she pulled on my sleeve and we headed down the slope a little until she suddenly came to a halt and held my arm tightly.

"Here, be careful as there are nettles and bracken as well. It's just down here but I think the entrance is more exposed." She whispered.

"How do you know all this?" I whispered back.

"Remember I was out looking for that buzzard the other week? I saw it flying and circling over here, so I came over and took a look. Lucky for us that I did as it would be so easy to have just walked into the nettle patch and shout out when you got stung by the leaves then caught on the briars!"

I was impressed and despite the circumstances, more in love with this wonderful person than ever before. Thank whatever god there was that we were together, especially now, I mused.

We carefully moved through the undergrowth until the ground levelled out and in the dim light the shrubs thinned, and we spotted the concrete end of the pipe.

I was about to let out a sigh of relief when suddenly a bright search light illuminated the treetops off to our upper left and we froze as we ducked down onto the ground.

"Shit." I said as quietly as I could, but we carefully slid along the ground as I hoped to every god I could think of that we'd miss the nettles and briars.

Then the light swung off towards the village and, through the foliage, I could just see it sweep over what was our home and then the neighbours.

Oh God! I spotted the same creatures as before and they were coming from number 12 and flung two people into the awaiting container/transport or whatever it was.

Mike and Sarah…

Again, there would have been no chance of someone surviving something like that. I wanted to be sick but forced the bile back down.

Simone hissed at me about something and I realised she'd found her way to the front of the pipe a bit lower down as I heard a faint splashing sound. I just hoped the aliens didn't have super hearing.

I made my way down, around to the front of the drainage pipe and in the faint moonlight Simone was trying to get the grill off it. I looked at the size of it and had to admit we would only just squeeze into it, then cursed myself for not helping her.

Together we pulled at the grill but to no avail until I saw the eight bolts and my heart saddened at the sight of them. Until I realised the kids had got to them and they were all loose except for two. Quickly we undid the loose six then I fished into my trouser pocket and pulled out my jack of all trade's Swiss army knife. It was a present from Simone when she'd had to go to Lucerne in Switzerland a few years back and it had everything on it - something for all occasions it seemed. I always kept it on me, but it was something I always knew I had because it was so bloody heavy!

But now that didn't matter as we could hear something in the distance. It sounded like the direction of our home and I suddenly thought about dogs and scent.

What if they didn't use thermal imaging but instead their equivalent of sniffer dogs?

I dreaded to think what sort of animal it could be, but it redoubled my efforts to use the knife to prize the final two bolts loose and then between us we pulled off the grill.

To do so we had to stand in the small 'stream' that issued from the pipe and I realised that the flow of the water was erasing our footprints in the stream bed, so I beckoned to Simone to scramble in as I looked around with a mad idea.

With the Swiss army knife I cut several nearby bushes off as I made sure the cut branches were not easily identifiable and, as I now scrambled into the pipe, my heart leapt as the searchlight again swung across the treetops, too close for comfort. I pushed the shrubs into the stream bed to make it look as though they'd grown there and pulled the grill back into place hoping it wouldn't fall. One of the bushes fell over but fortunately against the grill and as I heard Simone grunting, wriggling and splashing back further into the pipe, I too started to back up keeping my eyes on the grill. The darkness was suffocating, and I was again in awe of Simone as she normally hated the dark, but I guess 'needs must'.

Suddenly the ground and stream in front of the grill and makeshift bushes became illuminated and my heart leapt into my mouth as I froze with nowhere else to go.

This was it, we had been discovered.

7: Limp

The end of the tunnel went dark and I waited. Simone had frozen too and together we held our breath. Just as well considering the smell and the dank water we found ourselves partially lying in. I couldn't help but think that there could be all sorts of things down in the pipe.

Dead rats, indeed, anything that may have died and been swept down into the drainage pipe from who knows where. But it was better than the fate that had befallen our dear friends and their families.

With the phone networks also down, we had not been able to contact any of our own family members who were mainly based in Shropshire, Shawbury in fact, over a hundred miles away. My heart sank as I considered that they had probably also fallen victim to the aliens. I had to stop thinking like that. We had more pressing matters to deal with. How long should we stay cooped up in that cesspit of a drainage pipe?

I suddenly thought about the rucksacks and hoped they were not dipping into the water and so becoming contaminated. I couldn't reach back no matter how I tried and dare not say anything or switch my torch on lest the light was attracted back to the pipe entrance.

I knew we couldn't stay more than a day or so as the leaves on the bushes would start to die off and that would give away that something odd had taken place.

We had to move but for now we had no choice but to stay put and wait for a few hours at least before chancing moving out again.

I again reached back but this time felt around until I touched Simone and she grabbed my hand and squeezed it tight and I heard a little whimper from her direction. After a few minutes however, my arm began to tire being in such a strange position and I gently wriggled it then brought it back and into my fleece pocket as I fished out my smart phone. Hiding the screen as best I could I pressed the side switch and for a brief moment felt blinded as it came to life. Again, I desperately looked up towards the pipe entrance in fear that I had alerted 'them'.

Nothing happened so I glanced at the screen noting the battery was down to forty eight percent, so I was going to have to use it sparingly. The mapping app came up but with no network signal it could only display what was in the cache but that was good enough. We'd looked at the area whilst still in our home and I could see enough to get a fix on where we were and what direction we needed to head in.

Location services were off but knowing where our home was in relation to the pipe end, I could work out where to go. I turned it off completely to save the battery and turned to face Simone as best I could in the cramped conditions.

"My legs are killing me." I whispered. "But we'd best stay here for a couple of hours at least, then I'll crawl up to the entrance and take a look."

"Ok love. My back is also hurting, and my calves are on fire but, but..." She sounded as if she was crying quietly and again, I pushed my arm backwards and found her hand and squeezed it again for reassurance.

What must have been at least an hour or so later, my calves, back, feet and lots more were crying out in pain and I took the decision to move to the entrance. I did so and a fraction of a second later my right hand touched something slimy in the trickle of water and it moved, and I reacted, startled, banging my head on the pipe roof.

The frog or toad must have been just as shocked, at least I hoped it was one of those that I'd touched! I decided not to say anything. But Simone was crawling up rapidly behind me and I heard her whisper, asking what the matter was.

"Frog or toad in the water." I replied as quietly as I could, and she sort of guffawed in a stifled sort of way.

I slowly drew up to the entrance and looked through the grill and could just make out the undergrowth and the small stream that carried on from where the pipe stopped.

Nothing.

Silent.

Perhaps a little rustle from the treetops with a breeze running through them.

I waited a little longer, then, as carefully as I could, I gripped the grill and pushed it.

Nothing happened and my heart began to race. Had they realised and somehow with that earlier light sealed it so we couldn't get out?

It couldn't be, I reasoned and pushed again, then realised the bush that had fallen against the grill was acting like a wedge and keeping it in place. Along with the fact that when we'd taken it off in the first place Simone was helping. Now it was just me and I realised it was heavier than I'd thought.

So, I pushed harder, then suddenly it gave way falling, making a loud splash and I again froze with fear.

"Quickly, let's go!" I called to Simone as quietly as I could, and we scrambled out but the pain in our bodies sent us both writhing to the ditch side.

Damned muscle cramp!

I had to get control and forced myself through the pain as Simone seemed to think likewise and together, we placed the grill back in place and I pushed the shrubs up against it in the hope that if 'they' did take another look then it would still look undisturbed.

That done, I stopped and thought hard about the map I had consulted earlier and motioned in the weak moonlight downstream, fortunately under the tree tops cover still, so that was a blessing. Simone was right behind me but again I heard a whimper, but then, who wouldn't under the circumstances?

If I'd paid more attention to how she was walking, then I would have seen her limping with a pained grimace on her face...

8: A view to die for?

We steadily made our way under the tree cover, slowly, painfully slowly making our way uphill at a slight angle to the ground slope but avoiding any areas that looked like the tree cover was thinning. I couldn't help thinking back to what we'd read when buying our new home in what was then the brand-new village of Woldsfield. There had been quite a battle between the developers and local environmentalists who had in the end succeeded in preserving most of the nearby ancient woodland as it was considered an area of outstanding natural beauty.

Without it, we would probably be dead by now and I for once was only too grateful to those protestors, although now there was a chance, they were all dead anyway.

A sobering thought.

We followed a faint trace of an animal track, either foxes or perhaps badgers, although most of the latter had been killed off in a doomed attempt to blame them for the TB problems found in the local cattle population. I briefly mourned how scientific studies in a large swath of human made problems had been swept aside simply to appease certain powerful lobbyists.

It seemed ironic that it would appear that the human race itself was now being swept away in the same way by beings far more powerful than ourselves and with little regard to the so called dominant species on Earth.

Earth.

The Fragility of Existence

The Pale Blue Dot, as coined by the late American astronomer Dr Carl Sagan who'd recognised just how fragile our little planet was. Pity that some influential members of the human race didn't seem to grasp how fragile our ecosystem was.

Still, back to the present, and I began to realise that Simone always took up the rear, so I turned to her as we took a brief rest.

"Whassup? You OK?" I inquired.

She looked at me as if I was an idiot.

"Err, Matt, for flipping hecks sake, we're on the run from nasty alien things, friends and family are probably dead, the world seems to be ending and we're on a fool's errand to try to get to somewhere that we don't even know still exists or even whether we can get in or not. Wassup, he asks, Jesus bloody Christ what a question… OWW!" She finished with an exclamation and I saw her lift her right foot up and hold it whilst grabbing me for support as she winced.

"What's going on?" I asked as she tried to get a better look at her foot, but she quickly put it down.

"Oh, I just caught it a while ago and I've probably just sprained it lightly. Look let's keep moving, can't be good for us to stop in one place for any length of time."

Simone put her foot down and started to walk, taking the lead and I noticed the limp but didn't think any more about it based on what she'd just said. I hesitated then started after her but even under our dire circumstances I had to admire her from behind. It was later that I would realise love had blinded me to what should have been obvious.

The Fragility of Existence

We trudged on for what must have been another hour or so and I estimated we had to be getting close to our destination when suddenly we both heard a crack ahead as if a large twig had been trodden on. The sky was by now getting much lighter and dawn was soon to break so we needed to hurry. We both ducked down and froze, hardly daring to breath, as we hid behind what looked to be a gorse bush, with all its prickles so we didn't get too close to it.

Something was moving further along the dirt track and another twig cracked underfoot. I couldn't help thinking that if it were the aliens then they had to be deaf and again there was a sound suggesting something was heading our way.

Oh hell, this could be it, I remember thinking and we braced ourselves.

Suddenly a large, magnificent stag was startled by a distant noise and bolted past us and out of view.

The new noise up ahead sounded like a car!

For heaven's sake I suddenly felt stupid as I began to wonder if we'd been mistaken and there were others fighting back or also trying to escape to the bunker.

That thought was short lived for, just as we spotted something like a car headlights driving in the distance through the tree line suddenly a blinding flash erupted; there was an awful sound as the engine suddenly stopped in the strangest sounding way. We stayed hidden and I became aware that something dark and large was above the tree tops then appeared to move away southwards and disappeared into the distance.

We stayed still, not daring to move as I realised the Moon was now low in the western sky, setting, and I then remembered that there was a rough driveway leading up towards the site of the old bunker the Rockstar had gone to great lengths to buy.

So, someone else must have been trying to get to it, I thought.

But didn't make it.

My mind switched gear as Simone snuggled up to me and whispered.

"Do you think the aliens know about the bunker?"

"Not sure, could be but then they seemed to have destroyed whatever it was on the rough road up ahead, then gone. I'd have thought they'd have carried on and done the same to the bunker if they knew about it."

"Perhaps there's still hope then as I haven't a clue where we can go to if it is destroyed." She said and I had to agree with her. Of course, there was always the awful possibility they had found the bunker first and it was already destroyed.

We waited a little longer to be on the safe side before I carefully stood up and motioned to Simone to follow. We moved cautiously, still following the faint track, then carefully we emerged out onto the dirt road.

The sight before us made us both retch into the nearby bushes.

Clearly something like an SUV was squashed flat and pushed into the road's surface by such force that there had to be no hope for the driver or any possible passengers.

The wreckage protruded just a few inches above ground level and as I circled round, I saw it.

The remains of an arm hanging limply and almost two dimensional with blood splattered forcefully out in all direction from it. The roof of the car and its door had clearly crushed the occupant, the driver, but their arm must have been hanging out the supposedly open car door window and it was almost severed. The remains of the fingers had multitudes of squashed gold and silver rings on them and it seemed patently obvious that it was the Rockstar himself.

Deceased.

Then I saw it.

Some form of small remote control had been thrown clear and I dashed over quickly picking it up. He must have dropped it a fraction of a second before being killed and it was in one piece.

I looked further up the rough roadway and noticed the road seemed to dip out of sight and there was something concrete up ahead just visible in the shrubs and my heart began to race as I beckoned to Simone and pointed towards it.

Grabbing the remote, together we rushed along the road and down the dip to be confronted with what looked like a heavy steel doorway large enough for a vehicle and, as we approached, I pressed the small red button in the hope that it was the right one. The doorway slid open and we ran inside deliriously as we had made it! I pressed the green button and the heavy steel door slide shut with a satisfying clunk.

Simone looked at me and burst into tears as she virtually jumped into my arms and we spun around ecstatic that we had made it, hopefully to some form of safety.

We cartwheeled around until suddenly we were brought back to reality with a shock as we both stared down the barrel of a shotgun accompanied by a loud shout.

"WHO THE HELL ARE YOU?"

9: *Clarice*

We stood in shock but also with amazement and intense pleasure at seeing another human being, alive.

Even if the woman was pointing the shotgun at us shakily, clearly in a state of shock. We automatically put our hands in the air and for a moment I couldn't speak. Well, I'd never in my life had a shotgun thrust in my face before and once again I was ready to crap myself.

It was Simone who found her tongue first.

"We're trying to find somewhere safe. From them things, you know, the aliens destroying everything and capturing everyone they find. I'm Simone and this is my husband, Matt. We're from Woldsfield, or what's left of it."

The woman's eyes darted back and forth between us and she looked terrified, then burst into tears and sank to the floor dropping the shotgun. Thankfully it didn't go off. As Simone rushed over to her to help her up, I picked up the gun and inspected it.

It wasn't loaded, that was a relief I can tell you.

"They, they killed him, Rick, they killed him, and I saw it on the screen. I, I rushed up here to find the door opening and thought it was my turn." She blurted out then sobbed her heart out as she recalled the awful moment when she'd seen it all happen.

I looked around, saw the inner doorway, so beckoned to Simone and between us we helped the young woman up.

She, in turn, nodded towards the doorway.

We passed through one that looked as if it belonged in a bank as it seemed pretty heavy and had a strong looking seal around it. It led into a short corridor which had a round stairwell descending to presumably the other level of the bunker but fortunately, next to it, was a lift.

The woman, who still didn't give her name but seemed to be withdrawn, pressed a button and the door opened. We stepped in and she finally stood on her own two feet unaided and brushed herself down before shaking her head as if to clear it. There were six levels marked! She pressed for the next floor down and we felt the lift start to fall silently and it had to be said, very smoothly.

"I'm sorry about earlier, but after what I saw I was terrified when the outer doors were activated. I'm Clarice." She said hesitantly, clearly affected by her ordeal. Simone looked at me quickly then turned back to Clarice.

"Clarice, as in Rick Gandola's girlfriend?"

"Yeah, his fiancée or at least I was until, until…" She burst into tears again and Simone put her arm around her.

The lift stopped and the doors opened to reveal what in normal circumstances was a living room/lounge and she stepped out quickly followed by Simone and I. Clarice went over to a set of drawers and opened one, picking out a box of tissues and taking one to dry her eyes.

We stood quietly, not knowing what to say under the circumstances. I'm sure Simone felt the same but couldn't believe what the bunker looked like.

Clarice beckoned for us to sit on the large, sumptuous sofa as she took the smaller but just as luxurious chair and we all sat down. She again looked us over with those distraught eyes and I so wanted to take her in my arms and tell her it would be OK.

Although of course it wouldn't and I'm sure Simone wouldn't have appreciated the gesture no matter how well intentioned and innocent.

"Rick was obsessed with making sure any fans could be spotted if they came up here so had dozens of small autonomous cameras installed all around, mainly hidden in the trees and on the bunker as well. He'd managed to call before the networks failed and was coming back so I was looking out for him as well as watching what was happening to Woldsfield. It's beyond words!

I saw his SUV coming up on the cameras and was about to rush to the lift when there was a flash and that was it. When I opened my eyes the SUV was, was, ...flattened as if some enormous weight had dropped on it. I knew he was dead straight away and I must have collapsed or fainted. When I came round, I heard the inner alarm sounding. It was a failsafe that if someone managed to get the remote or break in through the main doors then if they didn't quickly deactivate the alarm it would alert us to someone illegally entering the bunker.

For a split second I thought he'd survived but I knew deep down what I'd seen, and no one could survive something like that. So, I grabbed Rick's gun from the case over there and came up not knowing if it was those 'creatures' or someone who'd survived.

Sorry if I scared you but I didn't know what to think." She looked down at her feet and sat gently shaking her head.

"Where have they come from? Why are they doing this? Why kill Rick?" Clarice began to sob again and just shook her head as she became inconsolable.

I looked at Simone and was also lost for words as I knew none of us had the answers. All I could think about at that moment was we seemed to be safe.

For now...

Simone got up and walked over to Clarice and put her arms around her as she tried to think of something to say. I looked about and spotted the very large TV on the wall; indeed, it practically covered the wall and I estimated it had to be top of the range and at least two meters wide by one and a half high. It showed a multitude of camera views of the outside and I could see the view Clarice had mentioned showing the flattened SUV. No wonder she was in such a bad state if she'd witnessed it live.

I quickly looked at the views for signs of the aliens but there was nothing and something inside me began to allow me to relax. I stood up, went over and found the off switch, no good staring at something like the flattened SUV to remind Clarice of what had happened so graphically in front of her eyes. Clarice just stared at the floor lost again in her world of despair, every so often tears would erupt, and she'd just keep shaking her head.

Finally, Simone came over and sat next to me looking tired and I knew the feeling.

Before we knew it, the events of the last couple of days had taken its toll and we fell asleep on the sofa cuddled together.

10: *Bunker*

I awoke with a start to find a blanket over me and to see Simone was next to me. We were lying on a luxurious king-sized bed and it became obvious that fatigue and recent events had taken its toll on the two of us. Clarice must have somehow brought us to the bed, but at this stage I had no idea what level we were on. The bunker seemed far larger than we had all been led to believe when Rick's plans had appeared in the local press.

Typical, all you needed was money, at least it used to be, money had not saved Rick from his fate and who knew what fate had in store for us. I looked over at Simone and, leaning over, gently kissed her on the forehead. She was deep asleep, but I did notice that her forehead was unusually warm. Mind you considering what we'd been through I was surprised we'd got this far without any serious mishap.

If only I'd had a brain…

She stirred and her eyelids fluttered open and she smiled at me then reality dawned on her and her smile faded just as quickly.

"It isn't a dream then?" She asked as she looked around at the strange sight of a bedroom deep underground.

I shook my head.

"Clarice must have brought us here - she's stronger than she looks." I offered then flung the blanket off and stood up.

"I'm going to have a lo.." I didn't finish as Clarice knocked on the door then entered slowly, presumably in case we had undressed or were doing something else, although thoughts of sex were far down the list of things to think about at this time and place.

"Sorry, I hope it was OK but you both quickly dropped off to sleep so I gathered you must have been on the go since the first night they attacked. Rick has a special wheelchair that he has to use… used to use before… well you know. It was for his mum before she passed away a few months back. So, I used it to get you both in here and hopefully comfortable."

"That's really good of you Clarice and we appreciate it, especially as we're strangers to you." Said Simone. "You're right, we haven't slept since it all happened so that was just what we needed."

Clarice walked over and sat on the end of the bed next to Simone and nodded.

"Tell you what, I'd best give you a tour as I can't imagine any of us leaving here any time soon and it's best if you know the lie of the bunker. I sort of hope there will be no one else as I'm not sure if we could cope with any more people. Rick had all this done because he was always afraid of the world and thought we'd be in a nuclear war by now. So, we're fully self-sufficient."

I shook my head. "What about power, food, how long do you think we can last? Water?

Sorry, I'm just trying to get my head round how much could be here that wasn't in the public domain."

Clarice smiled and nodded.

"Yes, Rick was paranoid about everything, said people were out to get him and the like. I just went along with it as, well you know, he was a rock star after all, and he chose me! He also wasn't the sort to take no for an answer and I hate to say it, but I suspect a few of the agreements about this place and probably other things were not above board, shall we say."

She stood up and as Simone did likewise, we followed Clarice out through the door to a short hallway where the lift and stairwell were located. I realised we were on the second floor down and Clarice pressed for the lift.

We stepped in and began the exploration of the bunker. Calling it that was an understatement if ever there was one. As she explained, at ground level was the automated steel sliding doors that allowed the only access to the outside world into the large garage, once the original upper floor of the bunker. The whole thing was built into the hill side with a smallish cylindrical shaft that emerged at the top of the hill sealed with a concrete cap since the 1970's.

The next floor down was the lounge with an extensive well stocked bar (nice, I thought to myself), toilet facilities and a small washroom. Then followed the floor with two spacious bedrooms with on suite facilities and a smaller room which Clarice explained was originally intended to be a child's bedroom if they had decided upon having children. She paused for a moment as it was clear she now knew that wouldn't happen and I'm sure Simone must have felt as I did, seeing the sadness in her eyes.

Below that was a huge kitchen and dining area that both Simone and I would have killed for, pardon the expression and circumstances. Off to one side, and to my mind deep into the heart of the hill we were under, lay an equally huge freezer and massive fridge, both fully stocked up. It was here that I noticed a slight hum under my feet and turned to Clarice. She saw the expression on my face.

"The power plant. I don't know what it is but there is no access to it from here and I haven't a clue how it works or for how long we can hold out. It's the same for the water supply. All I know is that Rick's music was liked by people high up in ESA and NASA and so has some sort of state-of-the-art water/air recycling system. Somewhere below us, deep underground, he's tapped into the water supply and it's purified before it gets to us.

It's really hard to take in that he was almost right, but it wasn't us killing each other but aliens. Aliens…" She shook her head almost lost in the thought.

"I know" Simone commented. "Of all the things possible, to be honest I wouldn't have seriously put aliens at the top to wipe us out. It was always just in the movies."

I sensed the mood changing so jumped in.

"Well, whatever happens for now it's us three and hopefully across the world there are other groups hanging on and somehow it will be like in the movies and we'll fight back." I tried to sound optimistic but deep down I simply didn't believe any of what I'd said.

11: *Not a good sign…*

We continued the tour as we once again entered the lift and we went down another level. The doors opened and we all stepped out. I noticed all the lights were activated as soon as we stepped into a level and I turned to Clarice.

"Do the lights go out if you stand still long enough?"

"Oh, no, they come on and stay on whilst someone is in the room. Something to do with thermal sensors and we all give off a heat signature. It means unless we actually command the lights to go off deliberately then they will stay on as long as we are in the room or on the level."

She called for lights off and they promptly plunged us into the blackest blackness I've ever known and I heard Simone gasp in astonishment. Clarice called lights on and once again we had full illumination, making us all blink at the brightness.

"This is what Rick called the medical centre. A bit optimistic really to call it that. We've never had to use it and there are only a few drugs such as painkillers down here over there in the cabinet. I thought it best to show you in case any of us get sick. There is a bed, but we have little in the way of surgical instruments as Rick always thought that he'd have someone brought in who would bring what they needed. He always thought his money could buy everything and everyone but that didn't work out did it!

Let's hope we don't have to use this level."

She looked at the both of us and grimaced then motioned to the lift. We headed down but I realised we had gone down two floors and I looked at Clarice, puzzled.

The door opened and again Simone and I gasped in astonishment as Clarice gave a little sweeping flourish of her arms.

It held an indoor swimming pool. Not full length but certainly enough for most people. Clarice just smiled. "Changing room off through the far door. It's not unisex as he didn't ask people down here. I've swum a few times, but Rick never got the chance to use his own pool..."

Simone put her arm around Clarice's shoulders and just nodded.

"Somehow it's all connected to the water purification system so it's constantly being refreshed. Seems such a waste of water and space but at least it can take our minds off things..."

Clarice turned and motioned to the lift and we all stepped back in. She pressed to go back up a level to the one we'd missed.

There was one more surprise.

The lift opened and the lights came on, but this room was full of computer monitors, very large ones at that, all covering the walls. In the middle of the large room was a desk and a computer with touch sensitive screen and icons all over it.

"Rick's control centre as he called it. I said he had connections with the space industry. From here every camera he had set up outside is linked to the screens covering the left wall and duplicated with the wall screen up in the lounge.

On the right-hand wall those screens are his special ones. They connect with live satellite feeds from all over the world.

The top row is what the major broadcasters are putting out so he could keep an eye on what the world is up to."

We looked at them, they were blank, not a single broadcaster around the world was on air...

Things didn't look good at all.

Clarice motioned to the second and third rows that showed the Earth from space and my guess was that they had to be geo-stationary and weather satellites to get the coverage showing the whole globe.

Most were still operating with the names of the satellite underneath. Five were tied into the various satellites that had polar orbits and could monitor the earth in higher detail. All showed our planet, but something was wrong.

The USA and indeed most of the Americas were no longer large expanses of green vegetation but were now a deep mustard or light brown colour. So was most of inland Europe, Russia, China and Australia. Mind you, Australia was always that colour if you ask me! It looked like the coastal regions seemed almost normal but then one of the closer orbiting satellites began to pass over one such area and we could see that the vegetation was dying off.

Even the usually stunning blue green oceans showed signs of being sick or contaminated with something.

I felt cold inside and could see the two women were also looking distressed.

"What's happening to us?" Asked Simone in a hushed tone.

"My guess is that whoever and whatever they may be, are converting the planet ready for their use." I didn't add that it pretty much signalled that we probably didn't have long left.

I motioned to the lift and we headed back into it, Clarice pressed for the second floor. I felt cold and empty inside with an oppressive feeling coming over me.

We were doomed.

12: Downhill slide

We sat in silence contemplating what we'd seen, and it was difficult, nay impossible, to draw any other conclusion.

Humans were finished. Despite all the rhetoric and overly optimistic movies, when it came down to it, we simply had not evolved intellectually and socially enough to unite the world and think seriously about how fragile and defenceless we were if we were visited by aliens. We always assumed we would find a way, somehow overcome incredible odds, but what was happening now was horrendous and on a planetary scale.

First order of the moment however was to rally confidence, so I suggested we ate, as I was famished. Ok, so it seems selfish and an odd thing to think about, but I remember some general or someone mentioning an army can't fight on an empty stomach. OK, we were not an army, I accept that.

We headed down to the kitchen level. Simone and I retrieved our rucksacks and laid out what we had on the kitchen surface. Clarice was impressed and we began to organise how our own meagre supplies would fit in with what Clarice had stocked up. After a while and a bit of cooking we finally ate our fill to use up the perishables we had brought.

Better to eat them than have them go off, especially as they had been in the rucksacks for a couple of days now and I was pretty sure we would not be able to go back outside to search for more.

With what Clarice had shown us, the kitchen fridge and freezer looked like it could keep us going for a few months if needed.

That was certainly a blessing, although to be frank, I personally couldn't see that we had a future. The good news, if you could call it that, was based on the bunkers outside camera coverage, as they showed no sign of the brown whatever it was that was covering vast swathes of the planetary landmasses in the satellite images.

My guess was that it wouldn't be too long before it arrived. We headed back up to the lounge and flopped down into the seats. It was Simone who had the awful thought.

"If that stuff gets down into the water supply then whatever it is could be poisonous so do you think we should store extra water supplies somewhere?"

Clarice thought for a moment then looked up. "Rick was into making wine and beer, so we've got loads of containers and barrels. They should do it surely?"

"Brilliant" I said. "We'd best fill as many of them as we can find just on the off chance. Great idea love." I pecked her on the cheek and Simone blushed a little as Clarice led us off back down to the kitchen level.

It took a couple of hours but by the end of it we had several hundred gallons of water stored up. Rick sure had been keen but like a lot of his other projects, apparently, he loved getting everything ready but often lost interest when the next thing or craze came along.

Lucky for us really.

So, we settled in and Clarice started to cheer up a little over the next few days, we gathered that it was down to her not being alone after all. Simone seemed to spend time chatting to her in Clarice's bedroom, I put it down to women talk but several times I did see her come back into what was now officially 'our' bedroom and I began to notice she was trying hard not to limp.

I had to ask.

"Everything all right Simone? You seem to be limping?"

She looked at me and I realised that she was wearing heavy makeup borrowed from Clarice. Under normal circumstances she did wear makeup along with foundation so it wasn't out of place and I figured now there were two women and a source of makeup it was only natural she'd want to start wearing it again since that awful tragic night when they came…

But now as she came close to me and sat down close on the edge of the bed, I noticed the tiny beads of sweat on her forehead again. I took her hand and it was cold and clammy and my worry increased.

"It's nothing…" she replied. "I've taken some painkillers that Clarice let me have. I did something to my right foot when we got down from the hiding place at home and I might have a little infection but now we're here I'm taking meds so don't worry." She said a little breathlessly.

"Don't worry, my arse! Come on, up on the bed and let me take a look." She knew by my tone not to argue and did as she was told. I examined her right foot on the underside. Near the heel was a gash.

It looked nasty. Despite her clever attempt to patch the cut up and use pop socks to hide it, the gash looked a terrible colour. Indeed, to my untrained eyes, possibly gangrene.

"For heaven's sake, Simone, this is bad. We need to get down to the medical level pronto."

"But it doesn't feel that bad now and I can put weight on it better. Anyhow, I'll just get a doctor's appointment in the morning and I'll be fine." She protested and seemed to be confused.

"You'll be lucky, love, you're forgetting the world seems to be ending and we're trapped down a converted World War two bunker!"

She looked at me puzzled, as if I was the mad one, then her expression changed, and she started nodding.

"Yeah, yeah, you're right. Don't know what got into me, of course, we're trapped. What are we going to do?"

I looked at her and kept it together, this was not like Simone, it was I who normally lost it if I was unwell. Yes, you could say a typical male thing, we always seem to make a mountain out of a molehill or claim we were dying from flu when it was just a cold.

But this was Simone, hard as rocks normally and didn't fall ill very often.

Together we headed off to the lift and down to the medical room as my mind whirled with awful thoughts and the fact Simone seemed to have a temperature.

I found a thermometer, you know, the ear type thing and put it in her ear then checked it.

100.2 degrees.

Shit, I thought. She was clearly perspiring despite the room temperature being quite cool and I realised that she was looking pale. Simone lay on the rudimentary bed and I bemoaned the fact that of all the things that the damned rock star had installed and kitted out, he had not seemed to have bothered about the equipment in the medical facility.

Facility! It could barely be called that. I looked through the various cabinets and single cool cabinet on the right-hand wall but the one thing I figured we needed right now was some form of antibiotic.

There were none.

I did find something that appeared to be liquid morphine so I measured out a couple of capfuls and gave her them in the hope it might do something, but I had no idea what the dosage should be so dare not give her anymore.

By now Clarice had come in search of us and the lift door opened, and she came in.

"What's happened?"

I explained as best I could, and Clarice went over to the bed and held Simone's left hand but by now she seemed to be drifting into a deep sleep.

"The morphine, you gave her a bit too much by the look of it. She's out for the count, but no harm done. Now if you'd given her the whole bottle…"

"But what can we do, I think her foot is going gangrene. She's got a temperature, 100.2 degrees, that can't be good?"

Clarice shook her head deep in thought and went over to one of the desks and pressed something.

"Rick may not have kitted this place out medically wise, but he did love his computers and smart tablets. He has got a software library that must have something that can guide us." She brought up a wall display and went over to it tapping the screen. Sure enough information and pages of charts and diagrams scrolled by as we both scanned the information.

After only ten minutes I sat down heavily and pondered the results. Clarice looked at me, clearly not sure of what to say. According to the info, Simone appeared to be in the early to mid-stages of Septicaemia. The gash must have been much deeper, and an infection had taken hold and was spreading. Only a strong antibiotic stood a chance of slowing it down but worse, probably even that couldn't halt it.

I cursed under my breath and Clarice looked at me uncertain as to what to say.

"We had to find a hiding place as we started through the woods at the back of our place and we ended up in the drainage pipe not too far from here. We thought we were on the verge of being found so managed to get in but there was dirty water and you saw the state of our clothes when we first arrived. It must have started then. God, if only we'd stayed at the house…"

"Yes, but you also said that the aliens did a second sweep to catch any stragglers, so you had no choice but to get away. I saw the second sweep of Woldsfield and they seemed more thorough as they… they found more people and carted them away."

I pondered the truth of this but there was no way I was going to just sit around whilst the love of my life drifted away. A plan was forming in my mind and I nodded.

"I'm just going down to check something on the screens. Am I right in thinking it's a single brief press then a longer press to go down to the lower levels in the lift?"

"Yes, what are you looking for?"

"I'll tell you when I know myself."

Clarice looked at me uncertain of what to say then just nodded and held Simone's hand again. "I'll be here with Simone then."

#

It struck me that the aliens had not picked up the energy usage of the various cameras Rick had installed all around his bunker, but I suspected they were such low power consumption and emission that they were probably not easy to detect. It also struck me that the bunker itself must be a power/ heat source yet somehow Rick must have also masked the energy signature as well so that at least gave me a little more hope. Even if it was likely to be only short term.

I was glad but now I needed to check something, if it was indeed possible. I quickly worked out how to switch to full screen mode for each camera and noted a couple seemed to have failed.

But now I was looking down towards the heart of Woldsfield and surveying it carefully.

Being a new village, it was quite regular in layout, but the planners had made a few changes to make it look a little older.

Something about giving it a sense of a past as a couple of the main streets were winding in nature. That was of no appeal to me now as I worked out where I thought I remembered where the pharmacy was located on the High Street, for want of a better word for the main thoroughfare.

My mind was made up and I tried to memorise the route but knew that it had to be on foot. That would lose valuable time but there seemed little option but to effectively reverse the route Simone and I had taken just a few days earlier. I headed back up to the medical centre almost lost in my thoughts and worries about Simone. Clarice had fetched a chair down from the kitchen and was sat near to Simone but was half asleep herself so suddenly came awake as I entered.

"You're going outside, aren't you?" She asked but in a sort of harsh, but understanding, way.

"Yes. I checked the village and have also looked for any signs of the browning effect, can't see anything so fingers crossed. The sooner I set off the better as I need to get back for Simone's sake."

"Then I reckon you need to be wrapped up as if it was a blizzard and have something on your head just in case. I think I know just what will help. Come on, Simone's going nowhere for the time being."

She led us back into the lift and to the bedroom floor and headed into her bedroom. I followed but was a little uneasy until I saw her go over to the fitted wardrobe (the very large wardrobe!).

Then opened it to reveal Ricks mass of clothes. She looked through and started throwing various trousers out, shirts, tops, thick socks, you name it, until there was a pile on the bed.

"Well don't just stand there, start trying some on! You'll need lots of layers in case that brown stuff does start to fall. I'm assuming you do really want to get back to us alive, don't you?"

She had a point and I ruffled through the clothes and started adding layers to my own. Three pairs of socks, two thin trousers with a pair of leather trousers over the top, three sweaters, two scarves and she found several pairs of motorcycle gloves which went with the final thick leather jacket to finish off.

I looked a right one, a larger version of the Michelin man that used to be on the TV adverts. I waddled as I followed her back into the lift, and we headed up to the garage on the ground floor. I figured if there was a motorcycle leathers then there had to be a bike and helmet to. Low and behold, Clarice went over to one side and fished out some thick leather boots and a helmet. I squeezed them on and made sure the scarves were fully covering my neck and making a seal of sorts. I clumsily looked round as there was something missing, and my heart sank as a realisation came over me.

I surely couldn't use a motorcycle anyway as it would be spotted or at the very least its sound and electrics would be detectable. That's probably how Ricks SUV had been spotted and I shuddered at the thought of what had become of him.

Clarice looked at me concerned. "I guess it's getting quite hot in there - hope you don't faint!"

"You're right but don't have time to think about it. Where's the motorbike then?"

"There isn't one."

"Sorry?"

"There isn't one. It was at the garage up near Lincoln, one of the garages on the outer circle road when all this happened. Rick took it up over a week ago and he was going to fetch a friend and go pick it up when he turned back before he was, well, you know the rest."

I looked around and felt an idiot. My heart sank again but Clarice had walked over to the wall on the left and pulled at a small handle. It swung open to reveal a couple of push bikes and I smiled.

"That'll do very nicely, I'll be knackered but at least I shouldn't be detectable electronically. I think just to be on the safe side you'd best go now but just show me the switch and let me have the remote control so I can get back in again." I closed the visor and suddenly found Clarice hugging me tight and almost squeezing the life out of me.

"Good luck." She said, handed me the remote control and then headed to the door and left me to ponder what would await me outside.

I pressed the remote and the steel doors opened, and I held my breath, hoping, nay, praying there was nothing outside waiting for this very moment...

13: *Woldsfield*

I cautiously kept looking around and above me, but the track was good. Despite being pretty much an atheist, as I passed the spot of the crushed SUV, I silently said a little prayer for Rick, before heading down the track as it wound its way under the tree leaf canopy. At least that would give some cover, then I remembered Rick had not been saved. The thought kept going through my mind was that he had been driving a vehicle which would have given off various electronic noise amongst other things.

I carried on and just a few minutes later I nervously joined the main road. All along the way I found cars abandoned with a few showing signs of the doors being ripped off, so I assumed the occupants hadn't stood a chance. A few were also flattened just like Rick's SUV and I dare not look at them as I cycled furiously past the carnage.

The thought of their fates sickened me to the core. I wound round the minor roads so that the buildings would give more cover and nervously kept looking out for any signs of 'them'. I reached a junction and then heard something. Looking round, I heaved a sigh of relief as a couple of dogs came running up to me and sat looking up expectantly. I realised that pets would probably not have been on the aliens take away menu and was about to head off when I spotted a few more heading my way.

I turned and started peddling again and saw the two dogs flank me, running along and I figured they were just pleased to see someone after all this time.

We carried on and I reached the High Street and slowed down only to find I was now surrounded by around twenty dogs.

This was a bit more unsettling as a few of them seemed to be foaming at the mouth and looking at me every so often. I shivered at the silly thought that I might make a good meal for them, then regretted thinking that immediately. Several seemed uncomfortably close behind me as I approached the pharmacy and I again slowed down, stopping outside the front of the smashed in doors. My heart sank at that sight, but I got off the bike, rather clumsily I have to add mainly due to the layers of clothes I was wearing.

I was also sweating profusely and looking about, decided I could risk taking the helmet off. The dogs just sat and watched me, all of them, their beady eyes fixated on my every move. Looking up a few shops down the street I spotted something that I figured might help out and I carefully walked with the bike a bit further as the dogs also got up and followed me. Now there was growling and a few gruffs from a small number of them, but undeterred, I stepped into the butchers. Just at that moment as I had the door open a cat suddenly shot out, froze for a second seeing the dogs then streaked away up the street.

It didn't get very far.

I couldn't look as the pack of dogs raced after it, surrounded then tore the poor thing apart. This, however gruesome, was my chance so I quickly went inside the butchers and grabbed several plastic boxes and despite the rancid nature, threw whatever meat I could find into them.

Insurance policy.

I found the door to the walk-in cold store so on an impulse as the meat in there was also getting pretty rancid, I laid out a trail of meat from the front entrance to the cold store and went back outside. The dogs had finished their gruesome feast but were fighting sporadically amongst themselves as there had been precious little on the poor cat.

I threw down the meat from the boxes in front of the open door and called out.

"Here boy!" Of course, I didn't care if any were female, but it worked and they raced towards me as I moved away from the door.

A thought occurred, what if they preferred something or someone alive now, they'd tasted fresh meat...

I didn't have to worry as they scoffed down the chunks then started to follow the trail inside and as a group, they gradually entered the cold store. Some started to fight the others off to get the choice chunks on offer.

They were in heaven.

Until I slammed the door shut on them and made sure it was sealed.

Time to get to work. I rushed back outside and over to the pharmacy once again. At first it didn't look good but on the second floor I found the locked cabinets where the more powerful and indeed dangerous drugs were kept under lock and key. No time for that and I smashed open the door.

No alarm went off as there was no power and I decided to just stuff as much of what looked useful as I could into my pockets.

The Fragility of Existence

For once, looking at the instructions was helpful, so I made sure I identified the antibiotics but also grabbed bandages and band aids just for good measure as well as various anti-bacterial creams for cuts.

Satisfied I turned then noticed the sky seemed to darken then go light again and I ducked down instinctively. I listened intently and thought I could detect a low-pitched hum which stated to fade off to the right so I slowly edged my way round the counter and along the wall until I could just peep out of the window.

Something HUGE slowly moved across the sky and seemed to stop. I held my breath knowing that my luck had run out and they'd found me. I couldn't believe that a single person was important enough for them to send it and I felt cold and to be frank, terrified.

I heard another noise, a baying and suddenly I realised that the dogs must have somehow got out - perhaps there had been a back entrance to the walk-in cold store for safety and they'd escaped. They would easily find my scent and I braced myself, death by dogs or by aliens, the outcome would be the same, so I just coiled up into a foetal position and silently began to cry.

A brilliant series of flashes lit up my eyelids.

So this is how I die…

I opened my eyes after a few moments as the flashes stopped. Then the low hum faded, and the sky seemed to lighten a little. I carefully crept back up to the window and peeked out.

The remains of the dogs smouldered away where they had been felled.

The spacecraft, or whatever it was, receded into the distance then vanished as I sat back down heavily and took several big lungsful of air with sheer relief.

I waited what must have been another hour just to make sure they had really gone then I got up onto my feet and headed downstairs to go fetch the bike.

Something clicked as I passed a mirror at the base of the stairway and I looked at the unshaven face that started back at me.

"Bloody hell, I really have gone to the dogs!" I laughed at the poor taste in jokes but then remembered to wrap the scarves around my neck and put the motorcycle helmet back on, making sure it was a tight fit.

Outside I picked up the bike and was just about to set off when something caught my eye.

It was snowing!

I looked again as we were still in late summer.

It was not white, but brown.

It finely coated the bike which had been left outside on the pavement.

"Oh heck!" I said to myself...

I rushed back inside and after a frantic search I located a drawer full of face masks. I took off the helmet and scarves, put three of the masks on for insurance, then put the scarves back on followed by the helmet with the visor down.

It was a bloody tight fit, but I didn't care about the discomfort, so I threw caution to the wind, dashed outside and grabbed the bike.

I pedalled like hell keeping my head down and hoping the layers would act like a filter.

This was bad. If this was the same brown stuff that we'd seen on the monitors coating the Americas and central Europe then our final days were probably closer than we thought.

I wondered, as I pedalled furiously, if the bunker was really fully sealed, but then realised that if Rick had been worried about nuclear fallout then it was a safe bet it would be OK. Well, let's face it, I had to think on the positive side otherwise…

So far it looked like a very light covering and I wondered if the huge craft had been the one to start the process. As I pondered this, I nearly missed the turnoff for the rough track to the bunker.

Thank heaven for whoever invented the gears for a bicycle, as going up the hill was a damn site harder than when I'd ridden down it. I passed the flattened SUV and approached the entrance. Clarice must have been on the lookout as the steel doors slide open and I entered and stopped inside the garage, and pulled the helmet off carefully throwing it towards the steel doors.

It had a thin filmy brown coating on it. I started to carefully take off the outer layers just as Clarice opened the inner door to the ground floor garage then stopped suddenly and stepped back in as quick as she could and closed it.

A red light appeared above the door which I'd not noticed when we had first arrived.

It was an ominous sign. I took off the 'dirty' leather jacket, trousers and boots paying very close attention to not touch their outer surfaces.

With the outer clothes removed the next layer appeared clear of the brown dust so I pulled out the various packages I'd salvaged and again carefully checked they had no brown dust on them, then placed them near the inner door. As a precaution I also took off the other extra layers and went back over to the door to open it.

She'd sealed it tight.

I stepped back, then shouted.

"For heaven's sake Clarice, I've taken off all the outer layers, let me in, I should be OK. The outer door is sealed so no more can get in."

I assumed she must have spotted the fine dust falling from the sky and panicked. I realised I could hear her crying, sobbing in fact and I banged on the door again.

"For crying out loud Clarice, I should be OK, I've checked over myself and there's nothing on the rest of my clothes."

"NO!" I heard her cry. She sounded like she was overreacting and was becoming hysterical.

"Stop this now, Simone needs what I've found without this stupid delay, get the door open NOW!"

"NO!"

I shook my head then realised one of the inner cameras was looking straight at me.

"Look, I'm going to do something, and I don't like doing it but it's necessary, you understand. Keep watching." I took a small step back and stripped out of my clothes all except for my underpants.

Cold, I waited.

It was colder than I realised, and I started shivering involuntarily.

I was about to go into a screaming fit when the door opened, and I rushed through carrying the medical supplies. Clarice was on the floor in a heap sobbing and shaking her head.

She looked up at me without acknowledging my state of undress and simply stared into my eyes.

"She's dead…"

Was all she could utter.

14: *Bereft*

It seemed like it had been hours but was only ten or so minutes. I had enough gumption about me to dash down to the bedroom and have a quick shower just in case I was actually contaminated then I joined Clarice down at the medical level.

I sank to my knees as I checked for a pulse, but Clarice was right, Simone had died.

Only an hour after I had left.

She'd had some form of massive seizing fit and convulsions which I was later to learn were her internal organs failing on a massive scale. Her symptoms must have been worse in the early stages but Simone, in true brave style, had managed to fight it, keep it hidden, until she could no longer do so.

I was lost.

Bereft.

No reason to continue with life.

I slumped down next to the medical bed and just began to sob my heart out. My Simone, the laughing, funny, tough woman I had fallen in love with was no longer there to hold my hand when things didn't turn out how I wanted. I was a child but when we first met, she had brought the man out from within my quiet shell.

She'd managed to keep going when she must have felt like the world was ending, which ironically enough, it was. My journey had been in vain and what was really kicking in the teeth was that instead I could have been there for her, should have been there for her, holding her hand as she lost the fight.

No matter what you say to me or think, it doesn't matter as I wasn't there for her in her final moments and that was going to stay with me for however long the rest of my life would last.

Clarice tried to talk to me, get me to go back up to the lounge area and try to stop blaming myself but I just sat there on the floor as I lost the reason and will to carry on.

#

Three days.

I sat there not moving for three days. I even wet myself, not caring a jot about such a mundane thing.

Three days.

Clarice tried her best to entice me with various meals she prepared but I just left them. It was a selfish thing to do and a crime under the circumstances considering what was happening outside.

Not that I took any notice of Clarice about the views the outside cameras were showing.

Three days of being selfish, arrogant and stupid.

No wonder I was starving. I guess it is always food that can be the most persuasive and to get you out of your depression. I also smelled awful, and Clarice even stopped coming down to see me. What was worse, I suspected that Simone was also deteriorating adding to the overriding awful odour and finally I snapped to my senses.

As quietly as I could I made my way to the bedroom Simone and I had shared, albeit so briefly.

I showered, dressed in fresh clothes, then realised I had lost track of time completely as it was almost three am. I knocked gently on Clarice's door and after a few knocks, just as I was about to give up, the door opened.

Clarice stood in a flimsy nightie but with a shawl wrapped around her. She looked nervously at me and I looked ashamedly down to avoid looking at her lovely figure.

"I'm sorry, so sorry." I said. Clarice burst into tears and wrapped her arms around me sobbing. Under other circumstances, feeling her bosom heaving against mine along with the sight of her would have excited me.

But not now.

I apologised again, then once again. We walked over, sat on the edge of her bed and she nodded in understanding.

"So, please tell me. What are we going to do with her?" She asked quietly.

"I'm not putting her outside, no way. I had an idea but I'm not sure you will like it. I think we should try to put her in the freezer."

Clarice gasped and put her hand over her mouth in shock.

"No, I couldn't do that, I'd never be able to go to the freezer again. Where would we store the food?"

I looked at her and shook my head. "We need to do something because she's, she's decomposing. Freezing her will stop that and stop her smelling the place out. She will also become a health hazard to us. Do you think I like the idea?

The only other option is to put her outside before the brown dust completely takes over I..."

Clarice didn't let me finish.

"You'd better come take a look at the monitors."

I could tell from her tone this was no time to argue with her. We headed down to the lowest level and as soon as I stepped in I could see what she meant and my heart sank even further.

The orbiting satellites still showed Earth.

Brown.

All the landmasses including the mountain ranges that should be white topped.

Brown.

Even the oceans now looked more like muddy water. Clarice motioned to the bunker cameras monitoring the outside and I was shocked beyond words.

Green vegetation such as the grass and the trees were dissolving, in some cases the trees were already just bare branches. Everything organic looked like it was being dissolved. She flipped through numerous views of the immediate surroundings of the bunker and it was desolate and horrifying at the same time.

Then she swapped to the interior view of the garage on the ground floor. The outer clothes, such as the leathers including the boots, were also virtually gone and just a thick brown sludge. Much like an oversized turd from an elephant lying on the concrete flooring. The inner garments I had discarded did seem to be OK, so I heaved a sigh of relief at that small sight.

"You sealed the inner door after I came in, didn't you?" I asked.

"Yeah, sealed tight so fingers crossed we should be OK, for now."

I looked at her, puzzled then something began to dawn on me as she continued.

"Our air will be OK, I think, but eventually whatever that is outside, will wash down into the ground and find its way into the aquifer that supplies the bunker. I'm not sure if the purifying systems will be able to deal with it."

We both sat there and took in the awful view and almost certain knowledge that there was no way we were getting out of this alive.

#

So, we did it.

We had to.

The most heart-breaking thing I had ever done in my life and how Clarice coped is beyond me. I still don't know how I coped either.

We emptied the large chest freezer and carefully placed the frozen food to one side on clean sheets from the bedrooms then, and this is the bit where we both felt sick to the core, we wrapped Simone up in sheeting. I found some plastic covers on the lowest level in a storeroom with spare monitors and computers. We wrapped Simone in them then managed to hoist her into the lift, up a couple of levels then over and into the freezer. We laid her out as best we could at the bottom of it, but it was a heart-breaking sight.

Layers of bed sheets then went over the top of the body with a final layer of the plastic before we then packed the frozen food back in as best, we could, moving some out to defrost to eat over the next few days.

Not that either of us had any stomach for eating after that.

After we had done, Clarice gave her apologies and quickly left grabbing the lift as I just stood and stared at the freezer, tears flowing down my cheeks as I bent over it, sobbing my heart out at how I felt I had let the love of my life down.

Ten minutes, half hour, I wasn't sure about the passage of time anymore, but I made my way back up to the bedrooms and as I headed into mine, I hesitated and almost knocked on Clarice's door. I stopped myself. Instead, I walked into our bedroom and slumped onto the bed exhausted.

I dropped off into a fitful and nightmare filled deep sleep.

15: Downhill

We did finally manage to eat something a couple of days later and over the following days Clarice and I resolved to put everything behind us and make the best of what we both knew was the worst-case scenario.

I spent quite a bit of the day just staring at the lounge monitors that I'd noticed on the very first day we'd made it into the bunker. The sight was depressing, yet horribly fascinating at the same time.

Clearly, I was being morbid and I couldn't help but think that the chap Simone, Jason, Caron and I had laughed at, not so long ago on the sea front, had been right.

For once.

"It's coming sooner than you think.
The End of the world is almost here.
Repent now and be saved for all eternity."

I wondered what had become of him and felt a strange feeling that someone who walked around with a board strapped to him proclaiming the world was about to end, *had actually been right*. I shuddered and couldn't help but think there was every chance he had also died in that first wave of attacks, if not then, probably in the second sweep that had narrowly missed Simone and myself but had claimed our neighbours, Mike and Sarah.

Clarice came into the lounge with a tray of sandwiches, and I realised it was roughly midday and I nodded at her and said thank you.

She just smiled as best she could, but it was clear our incarceration was taking its toll on her.

It dawned on me that she had not actually come to terms with her own grief. There was I, wallowing in my own self-pity and loss, when she too had lost the love of her life. What was more poignant, she had witnessed Rick's death live via the lounge monitors.

That had to be the toughest thing imaginable to endure.

I looked up into her face and realised she no longer applied any make up, yet without it she still had a lovely face and I smiled at her and patted the sofa next to me.

Ever since we placed Simone into the freezer, Clarice had kept her distance, probably out of respect for my feelings, but we were in this together and so I was glad when she did sit next to me and then take a plate for her sandwiches.

"Don't think much to the latest movie, do you?" She quietly quipped and I had to smirk.

"Don't make 'em like they used to..." I replied and looked over at her. She put on a brave face and smiled then looked up and her face changed to one of shock.

I quickly looked up at the monitors and what I saw made my heart bleed even more for the world we were losing.

A deer, probably from the estate just a few miles down the road from us, had staggered into the view of one of the monitors that showed the woods near to the bunker.

It was clearly in severe distress and kept trying to lie on the ground and scrape its back, backwards and forwards then rolling on its side back and forth. As it did so great chunks of its skin and muscle were becoming torn away as it was clear the brown dust was, in effect, dissolving the deer alive as we watched in sheer horror.

It was truly heart-breaking to see such a defenceless animal in so much agony and unable to understand or comprehend what was happening to it. As it writhed on the ground, Clarice started crying and rushed out of the lounge and I followed her as she raced to the lift sobbing her heart out. We stepped in and instinctively I held her as she buried her head into my chest, then the lift stopped, and the doors opened.

She rushed out and into her own room and continued into the on-suite bathroom. She threw up into the basin and I couldn't blame her. To see a living creature in such agony had turned my stomach but I'd manage to keep it in check, trying to look strong, despite the terrors I also felt about our circumstances.

I couldn't help but think it could have been my fate when I was outside…

Finished, she washed her face, came back into the bedroom and looked into my eyes so deeply that I felt myself blushing and she once again embraced me and held me tightly.

"I… I'm sorry about that, it was too much…"

"I know, you'd have to have a heart of stone not to have been affected so don't apologise. I wonder if we should turn off the outside monitors, it's highly doubtful there is anyone else local to us to have survived that stuff."

"Yeah. For now, I just want to lie down if you don't mind. It's trying to take it all in that I just keep finding overwhelming."

I nodded and was about to leave her in peace when she held my hand and looked at me with her bloodshot eyes.

"Stay, I mean, nothing, you know, but stay, won't you?"

I did as she asked and for a few hours all we did was snuggle up together and I reckon we both realised we simply needed to be held by someone. It's a powerful unspoken bond between two people that can, for a brief time, put aside the sheer horror of what we were living through. We eventually fell asleep and for once in the last few days I can't remember if I dreamt anything or had any nightmares.

That made a pleasant change.

Until just before I woke up.

#

"Hit the ball then Uncle Matt!"

I laughed at how bossy Samantha was as she and I stood on one side of the net facing her slightly older brother, Timothy and my lovely Simone. We were at the beach, it looked like the one at Andreby Creek and Simone and I were looking after Caron and Jason's children for the day.

The Fragility of Existence

We'd been to Skegness and on the various fun rides then moved up the coast. Chips and ice cream had been the order of the day and now we were playing netball on the beach with a makeshift net.

Timothy lunged for the ball but fell, however Simone tipped the ball over the net and I was too slow. Well, Samantha had distracted me by shouting out to hit it. We were laughing and having fun.

Then Sam, as she preferred to be called, turned in the oddest slow-motion way, looked me in the eye and said the most haunting words I think I had ever heard.

"Why did you let us die Uncle Matt?"

I awoke suddenly with tears streaming down my cheeks as the nightmare and the memory of seeing Sam, Timmy and their parents unceremoniously dumped in a container, rammed home.

I only just managed to bring myself under control. I was closely snuggled up to, with my arm wrapped around, Clarice and I shuddered as I wondered what Simone might have thought.

I was conflicted with emotion and, as Clarice remained sound asleep, I carefully extricated myself and went back up a level to the lounge. The monitors were still on and my eyes naturally flicked up to the one where we'd seen the deer.

No sign of it. Then something caught my eye on the fourth monitor and there it was, a large mound, completely covered in the brown stuff and I realised the poor thing was dead and being dissolved even as I watched.

The trees in the background had already lost their thinner, smaller branches and it was clear the bark must have sloughed off virtually all of them. Around the base of their trunks lay a thick pile of brown sludge like goo and again a tear trickled down my cheek. I headed back to the lift and down to look at the world view monitors.

Our beautiful world, blue, green and yes, brown in some places along with the white of the snow-capped mountains and the polar ice caps. That pale blue dot as it had been once called by a famous space scientist.

This Blue Marble, as NASA had dubbed it…
Gone.

Just brown coated landscapes clearly showing that not only the vegetation was mostly wiped out but the brown stuff or dust, whatever it was, coated everything. Then I realised something. Of the six global monitors, only three were showing anything and, as I watched, one of the close-up monitors lost the signal from the satellite it was linked to.

There could be several explanations, I figured.

It could be the effect of the dust locally on whatever the bunker relied on to get the signal such as its own receiving dish, wherever that was. Or the ground stations that the bunker was linked to, were the ones succumbing to the dust.

But the fact that three global monitors were still operating suggested otherwise. The satellites themselves were possibly malfunctioning or, and this is where I spotted something, another of the satellites lost its signal.

I realised the signal was not going off but the satellite was either being swallowed up by something larger than itself or they were being systematically taken out.

I guess if it was the latter then the aliens figured there was no one down on Earth to use them so why not remove them, clear the space, so to speak. Another view quickly faded on another monitor and I realised it probably was the latter scenario.

It didn't need an Einstein to work out there was only a handful left operating. We didn't have long, was all that kept going through my mind...

I headed back to the bedroom and Clarice was still asleep, so I carefully got back into bed and snuggled up to her as I tried to put the views on the monitors out of my mind.

I fell into a fitful sleep haunted by those images. I awoke to find her sitting at the end of the bed watching me and she blushed a little as I looked at her in her delicate nightie.

"Let's go down for a swim, eh? Take our minds off things for a while?" She suggested quietly.

It was a good idea and once down there we cast inhibitions aside and stripped off as we plunged into the water and swam playfully for what seemed like ages. At the end of it there was nothing like helping each other towel dry.

Yet we couldn't get past our thoughts of our lost partners/lovers and so we headed up to the kitchen level and set about making and having a meal. For some reason we seemed to keep from looking directly at each other, ashamed perhaps of our swim together.

Another couple of days passed and after getting up from yet another fretful sleep, I leaned over and gently kissed Clarice on the forehead.

"I'm going down for a swim, See you in twenty or so?"

"Okay, I'll probably have a shower, but I'll just have a few more minutes in bed. Not a lot to get up for." She added quietly.

I nodded, understanding the sentiment, headed out to the lift and even managed to whistle a tune, somewhat badly, it has to be said. But we had to keep our spirits up and I felt that under the circumstances Clarice and I could be a good couple.

Well, let's face it, probably the only couple, but deep at the back of my mind I kept hoping that there had to be others like us, holed up deep underground and that somehow, we would eventually emerge to step out on the surface again.

The lift door opened, and I stepped out but as the lights sprang into life I gasped in horror at the sight before me.

The swimming pool was now a ghastly sickly brown colour. Clearly the water purification system had failed.

Then the further implications of that thought struck home and I frantically hit the button to get back up to Clarice who was about to take a shower.

I had to stop her at all costs and the lift doors seemed to take forever to close, then I was heading up. I stepped out and immediately heard a cry from the nearest bedroom and I rushed in knowing it was the one we now shared.

Clarice was still in her nightie but hysterical and I rushed in not knowing what to expect and almost collided with her as she came out, shaking from head to foot.

"The , the water…"

I went in and our worst fear now confronted me.

The tap was flowing but there was a light brownish tinge to its normally colourless flow just like the swimming pool. She'd turned it on first before having a shower. She was incredibly lucky.

My heart sank as I took Clarice in my arms to console her.

16: Scrubber

I estimated that if we only used the water we'd stored for drinking then we could probably last weeks, nay, even months if we were really careful. Some food preparation would have to become somewhat modified in the process, but we could survive.

Survive, but for what sort of future?

If we let ourselves become morbid then I'm sure we would have topped ourselves, but something grew between us as the bond developed and somehow, we kept going. In the meantime, it was inevitable that we'd develop an intimate relationship. Who wouldn't, confined as we were with no chance of help or discovery.

We lay together in bed and it was clear that we'd moved on from our grief and now needed to live for the time we might have left. We coupled and managed to enjoy the moment as we cast away our fears and inhibitions, sorrow for past loved ones and the fate of the world.

For a few brief moments we cast all that aside.

We wandered down to the kitchen and made a hearty lunch and made sure we just took sips of water. One thing that at least didn't cause the problems I thought we'd have, was flushing the toilet. Regardless of what went into it from us, the water was now brown, so it all looked the same and we were relieved to find the water kept whatever the brown stuff was, contained. We just made sure nothing could splash up on us.

No flushing whilst sitting, became our motto.

So at least we didn't have to squander our precious, clean water to flush away our waste. Cooking was even more interesting since Clarice showed me Ricks extensive wine collection. Well, who wants to cook with water when the end of the human race was in progress. Who would be worried if we ended up drunk if we drank as much of the wine that went into the meals?

Perhaps that's why our inhibitions disappeared and eventually we couldn't be bothered to even get dressed, just wandered round in the au natural state. Who was to see us? Clarice had a gorgeous body, I could see what Rick saw in her and she didn't seem to mind, although I'm pretty sure the alcohol played a role.

However, we did decide to break our own rule and use a little of the water for a wash down. Which of course we happily did to each other, roughly every few days. No point in overdoing it and wasting a precious commodity.

Perhaps this was it, how it was supposed to finally end, and as the final monitors for both outside the bunker and watching the world finally stopped working, we turned to Ricks vast album and movie collections to keep our minds off things.

Until the power started to flicker one afternoon.

We were sat on the sofa, entwined of course, and I'd not given it any more thought since our first quick tour when Simone and I had arrived, but now a sense of urgency and fear crept back into our lives.

Rick had installed some sort of power supply that he'd obtained by fair means or perhaps by foul.

Unfortunately, Clarice had no idea of what it was and how it worked. Something to do with a NASA consortium. Somehow, we'd fallen into the trap of it always being there, so we'd not given it any more thought.

It faltered then picked up again, but it did make us more conscious of only using what we really needed. So, lights were always turned off until we went into a room and in the lower level we turned off all the computers that had been controlling the monitors. They were no longer needed so could be sacrificed. As long as the fridges had power and the kitchen then we could last.

I looked at the walls and shook my head, partially to try to clear it as I had a blinding headache come on over the last hour or so.

"You OK?" Clarice asked looking concerned, and I mentioned my headache. She looked at me oddly.

"So have I, come on in the last half hour or so. I'm not that surprised considering what we've drunk over the last few days."

I was sat mulling this all over with Clarice nestled into me and I stroked her thigh gently, when I had a horrible thought and without thinking I asked it out loud.

"Where and how do we get the air from to breathe?"

"NASA and ESA to thank for that." Clarice replied. "Rick had so many connections I simply couldn't keep up and he was fascinated with the idea of going to Mars or some other place in space.

So, he always looked into things that could recycle water, waste and purify the air.

He spent a fortune on this place as he was truly convinced we'd destroy ourselves. I suspect he gave backhanders to the establishment as I was stunned when he first brought me here."

I shuffled on my seat and looked into her eyes, OK, yes, I did look down at her breasts as well but come on, as far as we knew we were the last survivors. She didn't mind as it was clear she knew what was going on in my mind.

"So why were you here and not in some elaborate penthouse abroad in the sun?" I asked and she shook her head.

"Rick picked up on vibes coming from this ESA establishment somewhere in Germany, then from contacts within NASA. He didn't tell me everything until he'd brought me here. They'd picked up odd electronic noise that was nearby, I mean nearby to Earth and they knew it wasn't the Russians or Chinese or anyone else from here.

He was really concerned as several major heads of government in the west didn't take the experts seriously and couldn't conceive that we were literally about to experience the war of the worlds. They reckoned it was too farfetched so did nothing to prepare or bring it to the attention of the UN.

Rick made sure I came here on the pretence that he wanted us to test it out to make sure we were stocked up in case of World War three and I just thought it was a drill and one of his passing fads.

When reports came in of strange lights in the sky across the world, he decided to dash out to get his precious motorbike and grab some last-minute supplies and, well, well, that was it, he didn't…"

She welled up and started to cry and I shuffled closer and held her as best I could. I had wondered if she had been bottling up her grief and, what with the amount of wine we'd consumed, liquid and in our meals, I'm not surprised it all came to the surface.

Clarice settled down and shook her head.

"Who'd have thought it. He was right but for the wrong reasons." The power flickered again, and I shuddered as I felt it was sign.

"We should check the main computer, Rick only showed me it once and told me never to interfere with it but perhaps we need to look at it now?"

"Sorry? Main computer?" I asked puzzled. My head was a little light, but this new revelation caught me by surprise.

"Come with me."

I did as I was told but stayed slightly back as I watched Clarice walk towards the lift, the sway of her body mesmerising. I caught up and we stepped in, she pressed for the lowest level then when it reached it, I looked at her expectantly.

She pressed the button and kept pressing for what must have been ten seconds at least. The lift descended and I realised it went down another level or at least that's what I thought it would do but it carried on as if there had been two further levels. Rick must have spent a fortune on his bunker and not all of it legitimately.

We stopped and the doors opened.

Stepping out, the room was brightly lit and along one wall was a bank of flashing lights and a console in front of it. Clarice looked at me.

"I haven't a clue now. Any thoughts?"

I shook my head but sat down at the console and realised the screen was a touch screen, so I lightly wiped my hand across it.

For it to come alive.

But bloody hell did it look complex.

The good news was that it was showing that the air purifications system was based on NASA technology just as Clarice had said and that one of the 'scrubbers' needed replacing. I swiped the screen and moved that view to one side then saw a section with 'HELP' as a label, so I tapped on it and up sprung a mass of documents. Fortunately, you could do a search and I quickly found 'scrubbers'.

Good grief, they worked in the same way as the ones that needed repairing on that Apollo 13 mission to the moon donkeys years ago, but it also told me where to go get the new 'scrubber' and as I looked Clarice pointed at the display.

"Oh, that's what those things are, I nearly chucked them out but they're up on the monitors level and by the looks of it they go over there in the corner." She wandered off to the right and low and behold she tapped on a small latch and it opened up to reveal several tubular fittings and one was clearly badly off colour.

"Oh shit!" She cried and slammed it shut again to my surprise but the look of horror on her face gave me a clue.

It was clogged with the brown 'dust'.

"Shit. OK, we still need to change it. Is there something in here like a disposal chute or someway of us getting rid of it?" I asked and Clarice stood thinking for a moment before smiling and nodding.

"Leave it to me, I'll fetch the replacement and we still have some of that plastic sheeting left after, err, well, you know what."

I nodded, remembering what we had needed to do with Simone's body. Clarice disappeared into the lift as I went back to the screen to see if there was anything else that it could tell me.

There was.

And I didn't like the look of it.

We managed to change out the scrubber. Clarice brought down layers of clothing with scarves for our faces, balaclava's and thick gloves and together we pulled out the dirty one and replaced it with a new one. The only one, according to Clarice who was stunned that Rick had not bought more considering how carefully planned he was with the whole bunker. Perhaps he had not thought it would really ever need to be changed.

Fully wrapped up we took it up to the ground level garage and dumped it near to the door, carefully skirting round the remains of the leathers and clothing I'd used in my failed attempt to save Simone. My original garments had survived and so that was a little heartening but nevertheless we stood next to the security door, stripped off completely and threw the clothes into the middle of the room before going through and resealing the door.

We would have showered but with the water supply contaminated we had to hope we had nothing on us.

Next stop, the bedroom and throwing some clothes on, then we went down to the new lower level and the touch screen looked a lot better, thankfully.

We both also noticed we didn't have the headaches anymore so Clarice seemed pleased we had averted a crisis.

I didn't say anything of what I'd discovered.

That the other 3 scrubbers were almost clogged as well.

They clogged from the inside out, so you only got to see it visually when they were failing. If my appraisal of the data was correct, we just had a few more days left before the air would start to go stale, a build-up of carbon dioxide would occur, and we would suffocate.

We didn't have long left…

17: *Final days…*

I told her.

Well I had to, I couldn't keep something like that to myself and after a day had passed, we started to get the headaches again.

Then the power flickered a few times to add to our desperate worry, but at least it stabilised and for the moment stayed on.

We cuddled together and it was Clarice who pointed out what would happen with the air.

"I remember something about the planet Venus." She said. "A chap would occasionally come into the school when I was in the juniors and he would have models of the planets and gave talks about space. He always made it fun and he said something about the air of Venus being carbon monoxide, oh, no, it was dioxide, carbon dioxide. It is a heavy gas so there is so much of it on Venus that it makes it really hot, but is also very dense at the surface, enough to squash us all flat."

"So…" I prompted her to continue but I knew where she was going with it.

"So, it sinks to the lowest levels first and gradually builds up from there. I guess we'll be forced up to the ground level before the end. I don't know if I want to live that long…"

"I'm not one for considering suicide come what may." I quickly replied so as to divert her away from going into dangerous territory. But she did have a point and I had also been mulling the same thing over since I discovered the fate of the scrubbers.

"Tell you what, I'll go down to the lowest level and see what it is like." I went to get up.

"You're not going on your own, we're in this together and from now on we stick to each other like glue. If one of us looks like fainting, then it's up to the other to get both back to the lift and upstairs."

I smiled and looked deep into her eyes. Any other time we'd have fallen madly in love, but just being together and looking out for each other was enough, now the end seemed even closer than before.

Call it women's intuition, but she was right.

We barely got the lift doors closed back in time. As they had opened on the lowest level it was immediately obvious that the room was overly warm, but the air was suffocating and I quickly hit the door-closed button as we felt overwhelmingly suffocated. What good air in the lift had spilled out into the carbon dioxide filled room and we slumped to the floor desperately trying to get our breaths. The worst thing of course to be on the floor but in a panic, you don't always do the 'logical' thing do you!

Clarice had quickly hit the next floor button completely forgetting in her panic that she needed to hold the button for several seconds but then she clawed her way up the wall and held the button down and we began to ascend. The lift stopped at the indoor pool level, but I managed to stop her opening the doors as I quickly pressed for the next floor. We again collapsed in a heap on the floor, Clarice looking at me oddly before she fainted.

The doors opened and the gush of fresh air ˋ was *sooo* good! We gulped down the air and managed to stand up and she looked at me mystified.

"Why miss a floor? We could have died!"

"The next floor up was the pool and it was already contaminated. The dank air would probably have that brown stuff in any droplets so we might have made it worse."

She put her hand to her mouth then hugged me fiercely. "How long before we lose this level do you think?" She asked quietly and I just shook my head.

"I don't think we have long. We'd best go up to the bedrooms and move some sheets and blankets up to the lounge area. That should be the last level to become toxic to us."

We headed up and gathered what we needed. Once done, we headed down to the kitchen and did our best to prepare as much food that wouldn't spoil too easily out of refrigeration and took it up to the lounge.

We settled as best we could on the sprawling sofa, food close by and did the only thing we could. Watch old movies to pass our final hours or days away.

Musicals. Normally I wasn't that keen on them but we both sang and clapped and sobbed our way through many of the classics. Then a few of the recent animated hits making sure we avoided any that featured aliens. There was no way we could bear to watch anything like that under the circumstances.

The food started to dwindle as a couple of days past, then three. Perhaps the system had somehow automatically found a way of combating the fouling of the air and I began to wonder if we'd missed something.

We went down to the bedroom level for the toilet but on the fourth day as soon as the lift doors opened, we could tell the air was only just breathable and we headed back up to the lounge.

Rick had never considered that his underground bunker would end up being a tomb and we had to use the small wash basin he had in a small room to one side off the lounge. but he'd not thought of having a toilet installed on that level. Why would he when he had thought you'd always have access to the lower floors.

I had a stupid thought.

"Clarice, have you any writing paper?" She nodded and went over to one of the side cabinets and pulled open a drawer. Fishing out several sheets and a pen she brought them over to me and I sat down with them.

"I need to write something, vent myself, leave something just in case somehow someone somewhere has managed to survive and get to start civilisation again.

So, I sat and wrote:

Let this be a warning to you.
Yes you, you arrogant so and so's.
I'm talking to you from a position of knowledge, sheer fright, shock and helplessness.

If only we had broken free from superstition.
If only we had seen past race, colour, creed, superstition.
      If only we had united as one planet…

      But we didn't.

We didn't even have any time to realise our faults and mistakes and do something about them.
We didn't stand a remote 'cat in hells' chance.

When they came.

This is my warning to you.

Don't ignore it...

I furiously wrote out what I thought had happened and at the end of it, Clarice read it over and nodded.

We took it to the upper level but didn't go through the sealed door to the garage. Instead, we left it there on the floor next to the door on the virtually negligible chance someone or something might find it.

We headed back down to the lounge and settled down. On the fifth day we lay snuggled up together and tried to keep our eyes open. We dared not go to sleep in case we didn't wake up, but the food supply was getting low and some was beginning to go off as I also noticed I had a dense headache starting. By the looks on Clarice's face she had one as well.

A pretty bad sign...

We lay there and she just looked at me, kissed me on the lips gently.

"This is it, isn't it? No good going up to the garage level as we're only putting off the inevitable." She lifted herself up on one elbow and gazed at me with a tear in her eye.

"I'm, I'm really glad you both found me. I know it hurt like hell to lose Simone but I would have gone crazy long before now if you had not been here.

In another time and place I would have liked to have known you before Rick but I'm so glad you are here now with me. My head is hurting, and I don't want to say any more, but I do love you Matt so keep holding me and if we go to sleep one last time and never wake up, I'm glad I'm with you."

Tears trickled down both our faces and I hugged her.

"Same for me. I know I loved Simone. But we have each other now and I have no regrets."

We said no more and sometime over the next few hours we both fell to sleep one last time.

18: *Where?*

Falling, flying, kaleidoscope full of colours. Simone, Clarice, Jason, Caron and their children.

A man wearing a board declaring the end of the world.

Darkness.
Falling
Darkness.

Light.
Blue sky and fluffy white and cream clouds.
Grass underneath.

Huh?

I sat up groggily and realised I was naked. Clarice lay next to me, also naked and for a moment I couldn't help but admire her body.

Then memories and thoughts swirled into my mind, and I looked about and started to cry.

"Bloody hell! We're alive!"

I couldn't believe it then I noticed Clarice stirring and I leaned over and gently kissed her on the cheek. Her eyes fluttered then closed against the light before opening again as she struggled to sit up.

She couldn't speak but tears flowed down her cheeks and I joined in as we both stood up and took in deep breaths and spread our arms wide as we spun round joyfully.

I don't know how long we did that for, but it felt good and we slowed down and just stood there looking at the grassy landscape with distant snow-capped mountains.

No signs of buildings or other life but at that moment we didn't care. The air was warm and smelled sooo good!

We were alive!

My tiny sceptical self, deep down did keep asking how it could be? We had seen the evidence for it with our own eyes. OK, we had relied on the monitors but surely none of it could have been faked? I then thought of Simone and sadness swept over me as I shed a few tears, but I knew I had to pull myself together.

A soft but deep voice spoke up behind us.

"Welcome, I am..

...I am glad..

to see you are…

awake..."

Clarice and I turned around and instinctively took a step, or was that three, back.

Whatever it was, was at least twelve feet high, strange triangular, no, even more sides to it, - five sided or more, with three eyes visible on its 'head'. One in the centre of the head but sunken in and as we watched it sort of blinked, well not blinked as there was no eyelid but something rapidly covered the eye then cleared. Then I noticed the side two eyes do the same and I suspected there were probably a couple more eyes at the back. I doubted you could sneak up on it. There was something like a set of gills or slits where we would have a nose and no obvious mouth.

Then I realised there was some form of opening under what we'd have called a chin and that was where the voice came from. There was a neck of sorts but not very thick and then the upper body…

Well that was also multisided with three arms and at the bottom a second multi jointed body segment with three legs sprouting from it.

We took another step back but it 'spoke' again.

"No afraid.

No need…

Afraid..

Do not be afraid, ahh, that is better.

Forgrive…Forgive the translatior, translator. It..

Learns as we speak.

Settle. Do not be afraid of me.

I was one who founded, found you.

Protected you.

Saved you.

You are licky, lucky.

Please, name you?"

We took another step or so back but the tilting of its head and the soft lilting tones of the voice had the desired effect and I felt myself calming down.

So, I spoke back as Clarice held tightly on to my left hand squeezing it in fear and trepidation.

"I am Matt, this is my…my companion, Clarice. Are we on Earth?"

The alien seemed to have learned some human gestures for it now shook its head slowly and this is when my earlier observation was confirmed, there were two more eyes at the back that briefly came into view.

"Welcomed, Mattz and Claricks.

Matt and Clariccee. Clarice.

No, this is not your former planet."

A chill ran down my spine at this description of our Earth and the alien sensed our fear.

"Safe now. No Earth, safe here. No xxxx@@@~~"&&& to harm you."

"Say what?" asked Clarice as she began to find an inner strength and her voice.

"No translation of their name." It replied. "Horrible things they are. Wipe out planets, life.. Scourgae? Scourge. We, too late. Cannot apologise, cannot apologise enough?

Sowrry. Sorry. Tiny word does not convey our sadness.

We move now.

Home for you.

New place for you."

It glanced around then spread all three arms with its fingers, I counted twelve of them on each hand, outstretched. "This we make for you. New home.

Come."

With that it turned to go then stopped and the rear eyes seemed to look deep into our souls for a moment. Without turning around, it again spoke.

"Magriszz. I, Magriszz. Friend."

It continued to walk away, and Clarice looked at me and shrugged so we started to follow. I again realised we were naked then it struck me that Magriszz wasn't naked as such but that there was something like a fine skin-tight material covering it.

Oddly, or should that really be no surprise under our own circumstances, but I could discern nothing that would resemble genitalia.

So there was no way we could know if Magriszz was male, female or something completely else, not that it really mattered you understand, I'm just a curious sort of person.

Alien…

We followed, nevertheless. No choice really was there!

No idea how far but it seemed to take ages but was probably only a few tens of minutes. Ahead we spotted something like a small village down in the valley next to a stream and my heart leapt, were there others also saved? This could prove embarrassing with our lack of attire!

The 'road' for want of a better word simply started on the outskirts of the village and Clarice and I both found the surface resembled tarmac, and hard on the bare feet. Several houses lay either side and ahead appeared to be a park with trees and grass and a large pond.

Magriszz stopped, then gestured around.

"Home now. All yours. Full facilts, facilities for you. Free to choose any… place, house, home. Coverings for you inside." The eyes seemed to look up and down us and I'm sure Clarice was just as uneasy at the way Magriszz looked us over.

"Are there others like us coming here?" I asked and Clarice sidled in closer to me and again took my hand.

"No. No others found. You, only. Sorry."

I found that hard to believe and I could sense Clarice was becoming upset. For a few moments on seeing the houses it had felt like there might have been others. But now despair swept over us.

"So sorry. We too late, only you. Please let us help with this new home and guide us to what to do to keep you safe. Choose home please."

I looked at Clarice and she looked at the few houses and then nodded to one on the left-hand side nearest the park. I agreed and together we went over to explore and make our decision.

Magriszz stayed outside. Just as well as there was no way he, she or it could have entered any of the homes anyway.

And so, we prepared to spend the rest of our lives on some other world with no one else to keep us company…

#

It was inevitable, we had everything we needed, food was always made available and Magriszz did her best, yes, we managed to discover that little bit of information.

Until another time she came to us as a 'he' and it transpired they could change their sex depending on circumstances and their own needs. We were given very little information about Magriszz's race except that they were very old. If I understood the translation right, over a billion years old and they explored the galaxy. They didn't war with anyone, not that they couldn't apparently but they could defend themselves, we were told.

Magriszz explained about the other strange aliens who apparently swarmed every few thousand years and used old technology to travel to new worlds to scrape it clean of any life before dying out.

I did ask that if they died out how could they start up again. Magriszz explained it to us on our regular get together in the park.

"They can leave seeds of themselves dormant on the planet they have taken over and after several thousand of what you term years, they develop and I believe you would say, hatch.

They are genetically programmed to seek out their stored star ships and for some reason we have not been able to discover, they then can fly from the old destroyed system to a new world and repeat the process. Somehow, they know to avoid our areas, so we believe the star ships in storage monitor and search for a new system to go to whilst avoiding us.

We too, keep our distance and only twice before have we had to defend a world we had got to first. We were too late to your system as they took a diversion from what we expected them to do and so we have wondered if their ships in storage have developed a new strategy.

If so, then it has not done them any good."

My own train of thought stopped for a second, paused as I took this in and just had to ask.

"Why is that then?"

Magriszz looked at me and I thought I saw something akin to a wry smile, if that were at all possible considering she/he didn't have lips.

"They had not done their homework. Life forms on your former planet didn't agree with them."

"Sorry? What?"

"For the first and it seems last time in their existence, they fed on something that was toxic to them…"

I didn't know what to say or think as I had a flashback to that very first frightening night.

I saw in in mind's eye a replay of seeing my close friends through the binocular as they and their children were unceremoniously dumped into a container. And them the memory of Mike and Sarah too...

Now I knew what their fate must have been even though I had suspected all that time. Suddenly I was retching my heart out just as Clarice came out to see us. She rushed up wondering what was wrong and it took a few moments for me to compose myself.

"I'll tell you when we're inside." Was all I could think to say to her, but she stayed with us and I turned to look at Magriszz who did that strange blinking with her/his eyes again and just stared back at me.

"What happened to those bad aliens?"

"They have been wiped out, completely. We can find no trace of them on your old planet and there seems to be no evidence that they left their seeds. Their ships are empty of life, running on automatic and remain in orbit but doing nothing.

In your words, they are now extinct."

Magriszz appeared to let that sink in and I nodded understanding.

"Serves them right!" Was all I could say before taking Clarice by the hand and heading back to 'our' house, lost in thought.

I then spent the next hour or so explaining as best I could to Clarice the fate of the human race and of our attackers...

The Fragility of Existence

#

To be fair to Magriszz and her kind, they had managed to replicate most of the things they had found in the underground bunker and so other than not having anyone else around or simple things like live TV or Internet we were able to live some sort of semblance to a life.

Weeks then months began to pass by and although we did deliberate on the matter, Clarice eventually fell pregnant, much to the amusement and interest of Magriszz. By now Magriszz was a male again, or what passed as a male in his species and spent many long hours with us talking of the Universe, how they came about and evolved past arrogance and their equivalent form of warfare. We knew we couldn't restart the human race but for all intents and purposes we could live out our lives and Magriszz promised us nothing would come to harm us.

Around the usual nine months or so later, Lucy joined us after what had been a difficult and to Magriszz, traumatic, pregnancy. As Clarice pointed out, it was she who had been pregnant so bore the pain, quite admirably I might add.

And so, on a distant planet, somewhere in the Milky Way galaxy, the last humans began to live out the remainder of their lives...

Epilogue

Magriszz looked at her companion with one eye closed in deep contemplation of what she was about to teach her student. Her other eyes continued to look at the scenario around them.

"My role here is very simple. I am to teach you about the race known as the 'Humans'. How much do you know already from the official data archives and my own work?"

Bickalexx bowed slightly in deference and indeed awe at having the honour of being assigned to such a powerful mentor as Megriszz.

"You have nurtured and indeed saved two such beings from almost certain extinguishment and they have been allowed to live in a small enclosure. This allowed you to perform intricate and unobtrusive studies of them and their behaviour."

"Very good, so far."

"Why were they the only ones found and what happened to the swarm?"

"As you know, the swarm have a very predictable pattern and they are genetically aware to keep clear of our species. However, something made them deviate from their normal course and routine and it was too late to save the fledgling human species from extinction. As for the humans we rescued, they were located in a deep underground dwelling. When we arrived and scanned for life, the planet had been transformed and was totally inhospitable to their form of life, however, the dwelling was almost completely self-contained but on the verge of its systems failing catastrophically.

The swarm had found everyone else and of course consumed them and all life on the planet including deep into the liquid they called oceans, but it is still a mystery as to why these two beings went undiscovered.

After all we found them."

"So, they are considered unique and need to be kept alive and preserved?" Offered Bickalexx.

"Yes, in a manor, yes. You are correct".

There was a long pause as Bickalexx waited for Magriszz to continue but they had now reached the place Magriszz wished to conduct their meeting.

"However, there is something you need to know." She turned to Bickalexx who stood next to her as they gazed down. "You have been assigned to me to learn about the humans, not simply for your research, but to take over caring and watching over them until they and their siblings finally pass away from natural causes."

"An honour, it is surely, but are you assigned to something else then?"

Magriszz now turned and looked at Bickalexx and something akin to a sad look formed on her face.

"My span is almost over, I am now close to my ninety third passage. In human terms, I am two hundred and sixty-five thousand, seven hundred and three rotations old. It is now time for someone else much younger to take on my role. You have been chosen."

Bickalexx appeared and was indeed stunned at this revelation.

"But... But... You must still have some time left; we live often for much longer than that. Why? Is there something wrong?"

"Nothing wrong, however for my remaining time I have a new calling and will end my span elsewhere in this galaxy. Hence the need for a replacement. Walk with me, please."

Bickalexx nodded and together they walked along the long room, stopping occasionally to admire the examples.

"We have encountered many races in just this one galaxy and the two neighbouring galaxies also show interesting signs of the spontaneity of life appearing anywhere if the condition are right. We have taken on the role over the last three rotations of the galaxy of caring for and nurturing where possible creatures that show encouraging signs of developing, not just intelligence, but of an all-embracing nature without unnecessary violence.

I need to confirm if you are willing to take on my particular role and continue my work here. Do you accept the offer?"

Bickalexx glowed inwardly and smiled, rapidly blinking all five eyes in a show of admiration, pride and honour for the privilege of being chosen.

"Yes, I accept the honour of being chosen and will solemnly undertake what is needed of me." Bickalexx bowed and clasped all three hands across each other in the traditional style of deference and humility.

Magriszz did likewise in acceptance. She held out a semi-transparent disk and indicated for Bickalexx to place her hand over the top. As she did so both hands were momentarily sealed together as one unit then the glow faded and both hands were once again separate.

"You are now bonded to the task at hand. Very good. Now you may learn the truth of the matter regarding the swarm and the humans."

Bickalexx stopped, somewhat puzzled.

"I am at a loss, the truth?"

"Yes, the truth, for we have kept an awful secret from the humans, and they must not be told. However, you need to be aware of all the facts as you continue my work.

The swarm did not deviate of their own volition. We misdirected them towards the planet the inhabitants called 'Earth'."

Magriszz let that sink in then continued.

"Our species have for a long time been dogged by the swarm even though they have some form of genetic tendency to keep clear of us. We keep clear of them and they do likewise. But over the last three swarms there appears to have begun a convergence which we calculated would lead to a clash between us in just a few dozen of our spans.

At the same time, we had been monitoring the rise of the humans on the third planet out from their star and we became quite concerned. They showed lots of promise but could not seem to contain their more violent tendencies both to their own kind and to the other life forms on their planet.

Our best minds concluded that although they would come close to destroying themselves without any help from us, there was still a strong possibility they would continue out into the stars with those violent passions still intact.

In short, they were the one possible race we have encountered that posed a potential problem in the future for us, other than the swarm.

Everyone else shares our 'peaceful existence and ideals' and so are part of the galactic family. The humans, despite some notable examples, were overall too dangerous.

They have another saying, or I should say 'had'.

Kill two birds with one stone."

Bickalexx was reeling from the revelations so far and just looked up at his mentor and Magriszz continued.

"The Swarm were a definite future threat, as were the Humans. We deliberately misguided the swarm ships to Earth knowing full well that once they fed on the indigenous life forms they would be doomed to extinction. And of course, in the process, the human threat would also be removed. A neat and necessary solution to our problems."

"We exterminated two other species?" spluttered Bickalexx in astonishment.

"It surprises you?"

"No, now I think of it, no, it was an elegant solution indeed. Problems need to be addressed and solved and so I have no concern with it. But I do have a question…

Why did we save two humans? Guilt?"

"Exactly, although they were a potential problem and it seems extravagant keeping them, letting them procreate and providing them with a 'home' was considered the right thing to do when we stumbled upon them. That is why you have been summoned here, as you know, no one is allowed entry without my express permission. You now take on that responsibility.

Each of these pedestals contain other examples from our past and are part of my work. You will continue to monitor all of them and ensure they remain viable until they have to be permanently preserved. Some continue but most have ceased and are now part of the collection.

I will go into more detail as I continue to train you but for now do you have any other questions?"

"Now I know some of the truth I hardly know where to begin."

"Are you aware that we have places like this on every primary homeworld?"

"EVERY?"

"Yes, so I have to amend my earlier comments and clarify. There are two humans and their two offspring here. But we discovered twenty thousand other survivors across their world hidden away in similar dwellings and in submersible craft deep in their waters. They are located in premises such as this and in similar numbers per each location on our primaries."

"And our small group here, they don't know?"

"No, and it should stay that way. The humans, when motivated, can be highly ingenious and it has to be said, devious so we felt they should be kept only in small quantities."

"Are they aware that they will be preserved as a unit when one or all comes to the end of their lives?"

"Again, no. You will not divulge this to them. It is simply your duty to maintain them in as close to their natural environment as possible. They do not need to know their ultimate fate."

"Very well. One last thing. Are they aware of our true scale?"

"No, I believe it would, in their words, freak them out."

Magriszz smiled and again she and Bickalexx crossed hands as they both turned and looked down on the small, suspended globe. Inside lay a planet suitably designed for human habitation where Matt, Clarice and their children happily lived out their lives, blissfully unaware of the wider scale of their existence, such it was for the remainder of the human race.

Magriszz and Bickalexx turned and walked out of the huge museum but glanced back to admire the rows of plinths with globes on them, each a species, a collection piece for posterity and an example of the *fragility of existence*.

The end

Authors Note

Many of the Sci Fi ideas for this novel and a few others planned have been brewing in my mind for a number of years. Sci Fi has usually been the main fiction reading material and some of the authors I have enjoyed over the years include Arthur C Clarke, Isaac Asimov, Edmund Cooper, A.E Van Vogt, and Alan Dean Foster. More recent authors have included the excellent Iain M. Banks, David Brin, Greg Bear and Stephen Baxter.

But who can't be but influenced by some of the old classics by H G Wells and Jules Verne and for the former I had always wanted to do my version of the world in danger but not a rip off of the classic 'War of the Worlds'

So 'The Fragility of Existence' is my little token and nod towards Well's classic and although short, I do hope it has been enjoyable.

Astrospace Fiction Newsletter

To keep up to date with the novels written by Paul Money under the Astrospace Fiction banner, then why not sign up to the newsletter.

Those signing up will be the first to receive a *free* mini novel: "Lord Shabernackles of Grasceby Manor".

So, if you want to know more about the James Hansone Ghost Mysteries or the science fiction novels from Astrospace Fiction, such as how to purchase them and where, or when the next book in each series will be released, then simply sign up and you'll be the first to informed. There will also be occasional competitions or a give-away so worth subscribing to see what may be on offer soon. Note your information will not be passed on to third parties.

Just head on over to the following link where you can enter your email to be added to the newsletter list.

Note I will not share your email with anybody, and it is only for keeping up to date with Astrospace Fiction books.

https://mailchi.mp/1c69765ddf7a/jameshansonegm -signup
Best wishes and see you soon: Paul M

The *last* Voyage of the StarVista 4

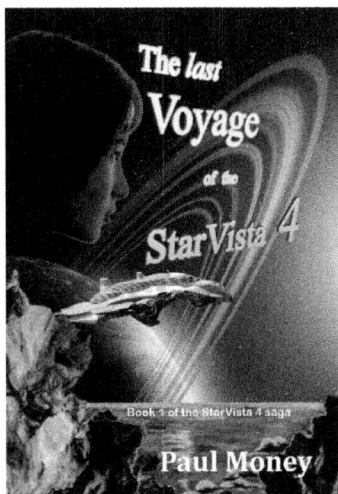

A Voyage of a lifetime. 2700 passengers and crew.
The diary of an eight-year-old passenger.
Stunning encounters with fabulous interstellar destinations.
The rings of the gas giant planet Tianca in the hardly explored Cantrara system.
A 100 year mystery in the making…

Follow the adventures of young Cherice Richmond, the youngest person allowed to undertake an eight-month star cruise on board the luxury star cruiser StarVista 4, with her parents, Carl and Natalie, the honourable newly appointed Earth Ambassadors to the Ziancan homeworld. Little do they know that they will never return…

Available on Amazon as Kindle, Paperback and Kindle Unlimited
Book 1 of a trilogy with Book 2: 'The Fate of the StarVista 4' coming soon.

The James Hansone Ghost Mysteries

It all started with a simple unplanned diversion, *'A Ghostly Diversion'*.

James Hansone is a computer and IT specialist and a complete sceptic when it came to all things paranormal. Until *that* diversion. It changes everything once he becomes intrigued with a ghostly face at a broken window of a rundown cottage, deep in the Lincolnshire countryside. Little did he know that he would go on to uncover the mystery of a missing girl that would change his life forever.

Now with four sequels, James Hansone unwittingly becomes a ghost hunter roped in to explore further mysteries with more books planned in the series.

A Ghostly Diversion
Secrets of Grasceby Manor
Return to De Grasceby Manor
James and the Air of Tragedy
The Haunting of Grasceby Rectory

All available as kindle, print on demand and Kindle Unlimited from Amazon.

Check out Paul's Amazon author page:
https://www.amazon.co.uk/Paul-L.-
Money/e/B003VNGE1M

Coming soon:
The Fragility of Survival
Book 2 of the 'Fragility' series

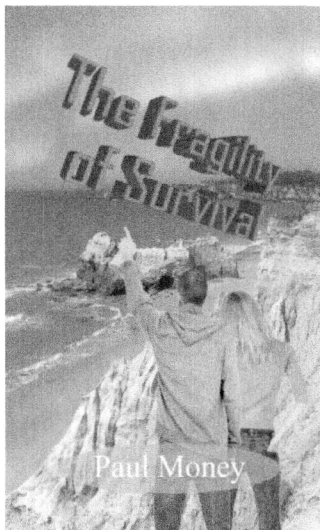

Holidaying in the Algarve region of Portugal was the norm for Scott, Katrina, Danny and Robyn.

Sun, Sea, Sand and well, yes, Sex, all played a part in their plans, but not necessarily in that order.

And all was going well until the world ended and two of the foursome became trapped in a local cave system, unaware of what was happening to their friends and indeed the world at large.

As they emerge into a desolate landscape, the fight for survival begins...

Coming soon to Amazon as Kindle, POD and Kindle Unlimited.

Coming soon:

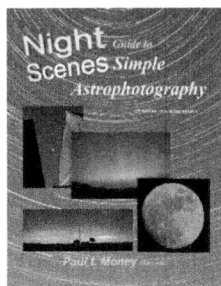

Nightscenes: Guide to Simple Astrophotography 2nd edition.

This book fills a space left by many astrophotography books by concentrating on only the astrophotography anyone can achieve with just a camera, set of lenses and a tripod. No telescope or complicated tracking mount required!

Topics covered include capturing: constellations, planets amongst the stars, lunar phases and eclipses, capturing the wonder that is the Northern Lights or Aurora plus lots more that can be achieved with just a basic set up of equipment.

This updated 2nd edition is larger format than its predecessor and includes many new images and new sections covering processing and smartphone astrophotography.

Coming soon to Kindle and Print on Demand via Amazon.

About the Author

Paul L Money is an astronomy, writer, public speaker, publisher and occasional broadcaster. He is also the Reviews Editor for the BBC Sky at Night magazine and for eight years until 2013 he was one of three Astronomers on the Omega Holidays Northern Lights Flights.

He is married to Lorraine whose hobby/interest is genealogy/ family history. As an astronomer Paul has been giving talks across the UK for over thirty years and was awarded the Eric Zuker award for services to astronomy in 2002 by the Federation of Astronomical Societies. In October 2012 he was awarded the 'Sir Arthur Clarke Lifetime Achievement Award, 2012' for his 'tireless promotion of astronomy and space to the public'.

His first novels were ghost stories: 'A Ghostly Diversion' followed by the sequel, 'Secrets of Grasceby Manor', then 'Return to De Grasceby Manor' followed in 2019 with 'James and the Air of Tragedy' in 2020 and 'The Haunting of Grasceby

Rectory in 2022 with at least two more planned in the series.

A first foray into the realms of Sci Fi saw the publication of this novel, 'The Fragility of Existence' in early 2019, a version of the 'end of the world' stories that seem popular. 'Fragility of Survival' is coming soon and is a standalone novel with 2 more in the 'Fragility' series in development.

'The *Last* Voyage of the StarVista 4' is the first novel to take place in the Galactic Arm Association (GAA) Universe, published in 2021 and several more are planned, one 'The Fate of the StarVista 4' will be a sequel due mid-2023, whilst a third (The Legacy of the StarVista 4) will follow in due course. Another novel almost fully written ('*This New Horizon*') will be the first of another trilogy whose story will eventually link up with the saga begun with 'The *Last* Voyage of StarVista 4'.

More info can be found at the Astrospace web site:
Astrospace/ Astrospace publications
http://www.astrospace.co.uk

November 2021/April 2023

Printed in Great Britain
by Amazon